WONDER

Also by

DOMINIQUE FORTIER

and translated by Sheila Fischman

On the Proper Use of Stars

WONDER

DOMINIQUE FORTIER

TRANSLATED BY SHEILA FISCHMAN

McClelland & Stewart

Library and Archives Canada Cataloguing in Publication

Fortier, Dominique, 1972-
[Larmes de saint Laurent. English]
Wonder / by Dominique Fortier ; translated by Sheila Fischman.

Translation of: Les larmes de saint Laurent.
ISBN 978-0-7710-4769-5

I. Fischman, Sheila II. Title. III. Title: Larmes de saint Laurent. English

PS8611.O7733L3713 2013   C843'.6   C2012-907767-4

Typeset in Caslon by M&S, Toronto
Printed and bound in the United States of America

McClelland & Stewart,
a division of Random House of Canada Limited,
a Penguin Random House Company
One Toronto Street, Suite 300
Toronto, Ontario
M5C 2V6
www.randomhouse.ca

1 2 3 4 5   18 17 16 15 14

We have the impression that deep down men don't know exactly what they are doing. They build with stones and they do not see that every move they make to set the stone in the mortar is accompanied by a shadow of a move that sets a shadow of a stone in a shadow of a mortar. And it is the shadow building that matters.

JEAN GIONO

Joy of Man's Desiring

—

ceiiinosssttuv

ROBERT HOOKE

De Potentia Restitutiva

MONSTERS

— AND —

MARVELS

It was snowing confetti on Saint-Pierre. Paper flakes flung by the handful from windows and balconies on rue Victor-Hugo settled in the palm fronds, on cobblestones, carriages, even in the nostrils of horses that shook their heads to get rid of them. Carried on the sea breeze they swirled for a moment before turning the shoulders of men dressed in skirts and bodices white. Powerful chocolate arms emerged from the ruffles and lace, and dropped veils over the hair of their lady friends, who were strolling along, waddling a little in pants held up loosely by suspenders of every colour. Every year, from the beginning of January till the end of February, Carnival came and turned everything upside down. Merchants, longshoremen, fruit sellers, fishermen, and women of easy virtue took to the streets on Shrove Sunday, staying there for the last three days of dancing, parading, and drinking. After a slow crescendo, the festivities culminated in an apotheosis that both crowned and ended the carnival at dawn on Ash Wednesday.

The rich and the powerful participated reluctantly in merrymaking they saw as a necessary evil, turning over the ballrooms of their mansions to their servants. But the poor took advantage of it to live for those few days a caricature of the existence they dreamed of all year long, and which their masters calculated – because they were allowed to borrow it, so to speak, for a few hours – they would continue to tolerate being deprived of the rest of the time.

"I am ridiculous," whispered Gaspard de La Chevrotière, stopping to gaze disdainfully at his reflection in the full-length mirror just outside the dining room, as if he were discovering some troublemaker who had, through trickery, gained entry to his house, and whom he had no idea how to get rid of.

"Which is the point of the exercise, my dear, if I'm not mistaken," replied his wife, who was prettily dressed as a chambermaid, and whose black skirt, white apron, and lace cap suited her remarkably well.

Baptiste (who at the time preferred the name Gabriel) was following the exchange from the table, lip-reading the reflections he could see in the big mirror.

"I can't button the trousers," grumbled the gentleman, pulling in his sizeable belly and lifting his jacket to reveal a waistband on which button and buttonhole were indeed separated by a significant gap. "Yet they are the ones I borrowed from George last year. It's utterly baffling. They must have shrunk. There is no other explanation."

"Quite so, my dear."

Before he was hired as a gardener's helper for the La Chevrotière household, Baptiste had held various positions that had brought him different sorts of dissatisfactions and vexations, mostly temporary, because he never stayed in one place very long. The previous year, he had even started to change his name, as one changes uniforms, when he took on a new trade, in the hope of some day finding one that would suit him perfectly. And so he had been successively a fisherman (with the name Lucien); assistant cook at the Hôtel Excelsior (where he was known as Jacquot); shellfish vendor; coachman (declaring his name to be Ludger); fruit-picker; and electrician's helper, that is, one of the volunteers responsible for carrying the tools of the engineers the city had hired to install the streetlamps that now lit the main roads in Saint-Pierre after sunset, leading some old folks to say that at this rate, it would soon be impossible to tell day from night. Under the name Auguste, he had occupied briefly the position of messenger boy for the newspaper *Les Colonies* and worked as a stevedore loading and unloading the ships that anchored in the port.

Of the humiliations he had suffered under his different identities, none could compare with the one he experienced that night, when he was served by Madame de La Chevrotière, her husband, and their lump of a son, all clad in uniforms borrowed from their servants, while he and the rest of the staff, decked out in worn silks and velvets loaned for the occasion, were fidgeting self-consciously on chairs in the dining room where the grand chandelier with its dangling prisms had been lit. The two valets, three chambermaids, the cook, and the gardener obviously shared his discomfort, even though they had lived through a similar farce in the preceding years and so knew better than he did what to expect.

Only Edgar the butler seemed totally at ease at this mockery of a meal, with the guests nervously examining their silverware as if the forks, spoons, and knives were liable to jump into their faces if they didn't pick them up in the right order or happened to cut their fish with a dessert knife, while those playing the role of servants balked at the thought of burning their fingers or being soiled by food destined to be eaten by others. The latter, like the former, tugged at their unaccustomed clothes , the maids going so far as to pity for an instant their mistress, who had to put on every day those pointed little court pumps that squashed their toes.

"The house where I was before, they gave us our day

off at carnival time," murmured Ninon, who was seated next to Baptiste, fiddling with a cameo on a black ribbon that was leaving a red mark around her neck. In her voice there was regret mixed with pride that could just as well mean that she would rather have been free to go down to the port with the crowd or that she was delighted to be part of festivities worthy of a lady. Baptiste, unable to decide which, nodded in reply.

Madame de La Chevrotière, followed by her son, Gontran, arrived with the soup, while Monsieur opened a bottle of Beaujolais with nonchalant elegance and served everyone, dripping purple drops onto the table-cloth that Marguerite, who served as laundress twice a week, regarded anxiously. "Many thanks, Madame, this is exquisite," remarked Lucien, the footman, politely dab-bing his lips after tasting the vegetable broth. Madame nodded graciously while the cook coughed discreetly into her hand. The three masters remained standing behind the table; all that could be heard was the clink of spoons on china and the sound made by Marcel, the gardener, as he slurped his soup. Finally, Ninon elbowed him in the ribs. The old man stopped eating and, looking unhappy, pushed away his half-full bowl.

At that moment, Monsieur plunked down in front of his servants a platter of fish that he then exhausted him-self serving with a fork and spoon, just as he'd seen his *maître d'hôtel* do a thousand times, never hesitating to blame the man for his awkwardness if by chance he discovered on his plate some grey scales or a long, pointed bone. After several minutes of battling the bream amid the muffled laughter of the guests, now jubilant from the wine, he gave up and decided to slice the creature into sections, which he placed with scant ceremony on everyone's plate. Baptiste, served last, was given the silvery head whose round eyes and open mouth seemed to express some unnamed surprise. After the fish, in swift succession arrived a dish of boiled vegetables and a puny chicken that Gontran, son and pride of the household, who had spent the first part of the meal surreptitiously guzzling a second bottle, served with all the offhandedness and reluctance possible, dropping as much bone and cartilage as meat onto the plates, and sending the peas rolling under the table.

The costumed servants were now laughing too loudly, showing their self-satisfaction and a lack of concern about being overheard by their masters, who were beginning to tire, unaccustomed as they were to standing for so long. Ninon and the other two chambermaids, dressed as grand *bourgeoises*, bit their lips to make the blood flow, turning them the vivid red so flattering to their complexions, and constantly leaned over to display charms set off by their low-cut necklines.

"Did you see her with that tureen?" sniffed the cook. "She looked like she was carrying a chamber pot."

From the street came the shouts and laughter of the crowd heading *en masse* to the port where they were preparing to throw King Vaval into the water. Each year, Vaval represented the greatest peril to have struck the island of Martinique and its inhabitants over the previous twelve months, or the greatest that threatened to occur during the following year, be it corrupt politician, bloodthirsty murderer, epidemic of fever or flu. The effigy was flung into the sea after a noisy procession punctuated by rattles and tambourines, all to the great displeasure of Father Blanchot who, ever since his arrival, had been fiercely opposed to these festivities, so reminiscent of the excesses of pagan bacchanalia.

Finally the meal was ending and the chocolate cake, crowning the feast, was brought in. Sated, fired up by alcohol but even more by the images in the mirrors of their flushed faces above lace collars, the guests spoke loudly, proposing toasts and, forgetting the silverware that had just a while ago caused them such anxiety, they grabbed handfuls of bread and fruit from their baskets. Edgar the butler – who, Baptiste observed, was the only one not in costume, maybe because, assuming that his status placed him somewhere between masters and servants, he had merely reversed one half of his person for another – gazed unruffled at the scene, while Madame de La Chevrotière busied herself cutting the cake, not without a certain dexterity.

"Here, my good man," she murmured, offering the first slice to Jacques, her first valet for more than twenty years now, as she would have offered a banknote to a beggar on the street. He took it with an awkward gesture and the plate, dropping from Madame's pudgy hands, shattered on the mahogany floor.

The comfortably seated guests now realized why their masters refused to get up or even to bend over whenever they happened to let fall an implement or their napkin. For their part, Monsieur and Madame had obviously no intention of getting down on hands and knees to pick up a mixture of sticky crumbs and sharp shards. As for Edgar, it would never have crossed his mind to lift a finger, each of his two halves transferring onto the other the responsibility to intervene; he became, if it were possible, even more stiff than before, approaching in fixedness the bronze Louis XVIII scornfully watching the table from a corner. The seated and the standing stared at each other in a silence where floated famines, suggestions of let-them-eat-cake, the threat of guillotines.

Baptiste pushed back his chair noisily and, saying "Madame" at once to both Madame de La Chevrotière, motionless amid the broken china, and the chambermaid at whose feet the plate had smashed, began to clean it up with his bare hands, as if he were gathering oyster shells on the beach. The next day at dawn he left the house without asking for his wages but taking with him two silver candlesticks.

When he shut the door behind him, the streets were still covered with confetti, while empty bottles testified to the merrymaking of the night before; on the waves floated the remains of the sacrificed effigy, which that year had been made to look like an American businessman who had stripped several of the Saint-Pierre widows of their fortunes before disappearing mysteriously. It would not have occurred to anyone to have constructed a King Vaval that depicted the very mountain in whose shadow the festivities were taking place for the last time.

SHORTLY AFTER THE END OF CARNIVAL, WHEN everyone had resumed his place and the streamers had lost the last of their colours in the gutters, Mount Pelée began to sputter, releasing some feeble clouds, grey or white, sometimes accompanied by brief tremors. No one on the island seemed disturbed by this, for people were accustomed to such benign events. Settled now in the village of Le Prêcheur where, calling himself Mathias, he'd become a coffee-picker, Baptiste had got in the habit of looking up several times a day at puffs of smoke that looked as if they'd escaped from the bowl of a giant pipe. It was only after three weeks of indistinct rumbling that, curious more than genuinely worried, he undertook to climb the mountain to see what was brewing in the mist around the peak.

When he was a child, he used to observe the peaceful contentment of families who went to the mountain for their Sunday stroll. He had often played with boys his age, climbing the slopes of Pelée all the way to Lac des

Palmistes, a round basin that provided tepid water to cool down in after the ascent. A metal cross stuck into the rim of the pool was reflected on the blue surface, casting a protective shadow that their splashing would briefly trouble. Other children canoed there or floated wooden boats that Baptiste looked at speechless, not even thinking about envying them. The sight of these family gatherings filled him with something like sorrow, and he soon discovered that he preferred the Étang Sec, a shrivelled crater several hundred metres below that had no water at any time and for that reason did not attract picnickers. He would stretch out on his back in the middle of the lunar circle, close his eyes, and it would seem to him that he was the last human on earth – or the first.

On the mountain's flanks, amid the jungle of palms, banana trees, and flowers, some of them with large petals swinging high above his head, the rock was pierced with vents from which escaped now and then putrid fumes that smelled of eggs left out in the sun. Those stinking holes were lined with the prettiest lace: festoons of red or ochre, concretions similar to those that grow secretly in the silence of grottoes, drop by drop, but here, in the sun of Martinique, they appeared overnight; purple or scarlet interlacing recalling the forests of coral hidden away in the depths of the sea, the crenellation so delicate it looked as if it would crumble at the slightest breath but that when touched proved to be as hard as rock; guipure lace of dazzling gold as bright as the scales of the plentiful yellowtail snapper that fisherman roasted over charcoal on the beach.

One day Baptiste had wanted to take one of the mineral flowers out of the rock from which it had blossomed. Reaching out delicately to grasp a petal between thumb and forefinger as if it were a butterfly he was afraid of frightening, he had discovered that the stone was blazing hot and hastily pulled away his hand. For a number of days he had on the pad of his thumb a nasty blister oozing a liquid as clear as water; eventually it was replaced by a pale scar with an irregular outline that recalled in miniature the stone rose he'd wanted to take away, its image now graven into his flesh like a punishment, a reward, or an omen.

In this month of March 1902, Mount Pelée was deserted and, as he was climbing, Baptiste felt the earth tremble under his feet, run through with long shivers. Arriving at the Cross he discovered, stupefied, that from the Étang Sec were rising not the wisps of vapour he was used to but abundant sulphur clouds that rose directly into the air, like jets of water bursting from the blowholes of whales. The acrid, burning mist stung his eyes, forcing him nearly to grope his way along. The phenomenon seemed to him spectacular enough to warrant his tracing onto the bare cliff in large indistinct letters the following words, using a piece of quartz that left an uneven line on the stone:

Today, March 23, the Étang Sec crater is erupting.

He reread slowly the white message on the grey surface and realized that he'd neglected to write the year. He wanted to add that piece of information, but stopped as if prompted by a kind of superstition. In truth, he would have felt he was writing his own epitaph.

· · · · · · · ·

When he left the village of Le Prêcheur to settle in Saint-Pierre a month later, he had grown a sparse beard and developed new calluses on his hands, not from the sharp edges of shells but from the varnished leaves of coffee trees; his hair and clothes had the woody aroma of the roasting greenish beans that would be infused to obtain a brew the pickers drank morning and night, scalding and thick as molasses. He also had banknotes in his pockets.

The night he came back to town, he went to the Blessé-Bobo tavern in the port and saw Gontran de La Chevrotière, who didn't recognize him. Leaning on the bar with associates dressed like himself in velvet and lace-trimmed shirts, everyone fairly tipsy and thrilled to be slumming like this, the popinjay was busy greeting each of his own rejoinders with a roar of laughter.

The room was crammed: sailors back on terra firma after long months at sea; clerks, vendors, and labourers from the area, here to spend their day's earnings on cool beer and spicy rum; a few tourists, white, black, brown, and beige men with courtesans' gowns forming bright spots amid the noisy and multicoloured mosaic. One of the girls, a mulatto with very brown skin and delicate features, was sitting at the bar, straight-backed, smile plastered on her lips, eyes alert, her slender waist hugged in a red dress with a flared, ruffled skirt like the corolla of a hibiscus blossom that begins to crumple as soon as it opens.

Gontran approached her, walking in what he hoped was a comical way, but hesitant because he was intoxicated; to the great amusement of his companions, he plunged his hand into the bodice of the young woman. She shook him off with one brisk movement but he grabbed her by the waist and, to hurrahs, planted a resounding kiss on her mouth. After Baptiste saw Gontran's fingers climb again up the flounces on the bright red skirt, he got up reflexively, felt in his belt for the knife he'd been using since childhood to open oysters, slice mangoes, and cut off the heads of fish, then noted the surprise painted on Gontran's face as the youth brought his hand to his side, where a red stain was spreading. Baptiste met the girl's gaze, at once incredulous and grateful; she had dropped her smile as if getting rid of a mask.

A circle formed rapidly around Gontran de La Chevrotière, stretched out on the ground, shrieking like a stuck pig, while Baptiste went calmly back to his seat, where he had time to finish his molasses beer before the gendarmes arrived to handcuff him.

He was assigned to a bright cell furnished with an iron bed where he spent idle days, sitting or lying down, following the activities of the police force, inhaling the smells from the port, and, most of all, through a window striped with broadly spaced bars, gazing out at the sea. Having discovered that the metal rods were set in a cement made of sand and crushed shells that the salt air turned to dust if it was rubbed even a little energetically, he quickly dislodged three bars, which allowed him to go out once night had fallen. He paced the streets, had a drink, looked at the girls, and came back before dawn, in time for the first inspection by the new guard starting his shift. At that time he was served a jug of cloudy water, a hunk of bread, and a thin soup with a few shrivelled scraps of vegetables, which he stretched out all day, knowing he'd get nothing else to eat. He would be careful to take sustenance during the night, but the alcohol he poured down his throat, which left a burning sensation in his gullet, gave him a cruel thirst, and more than once, without a thought of shame, he begged an indifferent guard to bring him something to drink – a request that was always ignored. At sunset, as soon as he had left his cell he rushed to the water tank next to the police station, plunged in the wooden spoon attached with a cord and took long swigs of sun-warmed water in which floated the smell of wood and sometimes a few whitish nits he later imagined with a shiver of disgust writhing in his stomach.

Why escape like that every night? Unquestionably because of his longing for freedom, a need to prove to himself that he was not exactly a prisoner, that although he was behind bars every morning it was partly because he had chosen confinement or at least was not its helpless victim. In that case why choose to come back and slip inside these four walls? Why not instead embark on a ship bound for Dominica or Saint Lucia, or simply walk to the village of Le Prêcheur? If he returned to his cell every morning it was not because he'd heard that Gontran de La Chevrotière had been operated on twice and hadn't yet started walking, nor because the girl hadn't come to see him, she who could have testified in his favour during the trial for which the date had not yet been set. Simply, when the dawn rose after his first nocturnal escape, when the sun was glowing red above the port, staining the sky with the pinks and purples seen in the cavities of shells, it had occurred to him that he had nowhere else to go.

"I'm confused," said the senior Monsieur de La Chevrotière, who then took a swig of Armagnac for comfort.

Sitting in a well-padded armchair in the stylish office of his friend and colleague La Tour-Major, he looked at the four men gathered around him, none of whom seemed to share his agitation. His mind at ease about the health of his son Gontran, who was still hospitalized but, he'd been assured, out of danger and would soon recover all his faculties – whatever that meant – he now had time to devote to more pressing matters, notably the election of his friend Charles-Zéphyrin de La Tour-Major to the position of deputy. Just then a muffled growling could be heard from outside and his fingers clenched the brocade armrest.

"Yet it couldn't be simpler, my dear fellow: we do nothing," said La Tour-Major, looking straight ahead and with a hint of irritation in his voice.

"I agree absolutely," said Edmond Desmarteaux in

the smug tone of one who has made a brave and difficult decision.

"But . . ." insisted La Chevrotière feebly, from a need to be reassured yet again rather than to raise a true objection, "is there really no danger?"

"None at all," confirmed La Tour-Major.

"None," repeated Desmarteaux, full of authority.

Mount Pelée had been rumbling for a while now, almost imperceptibly at first, then more and more loudly, until no one could ignore it, although nobody knew exactly when it had started. On the streets, in simple houses and elegant dwellings, from private clubs all the way to the gilded salons in the governor's residence, to the stalls in the port, to the ships arriving at or leaving the island, people commented with interest but with no particular fear on the events on the mountain, as they would have done for any meteorological phenomenon – a cloudburst, a hailstorm – or astronomical one – a comet or a lunar eclipse – seen as uncommon but not exceptional. For Mount Pelée had always been at the heart of the lives of the people of Martinique, accustomed whenever they turned their heads to finding its massive silhouette standing out against the horizon, a form as familiar as that of a big sleeping dog one might step over absentmindedly without thinking it could bite. Its very name testified to a kind of amused familiarity; it was peeled, that is bald, like the paunchy uncles or salesmen people pointed at, laughing, when their backs were turned, as bald as the governor under his wig in days gone by.

Admittedly, the volcano was neither dead nor extinguished, everyone knew that, but its bursts of activity were too rare, too weak, too decorative to be taken seriously. All the more so because this time they were happening in the midst of a crucial election campaign. It pitted Charles-Zéphyrin de La Tour-Major, a powerful white *béké* whose family had been in Martinique for three generations and owned nearly one-fifth of the land on the island, who had held the position of deputy on the General Council for twenty years and intended to give it over when the time came only to his son who, for the time being, was still in short pants, against Maurice Larue, an obscure individual from Saint-Pierre who'd been able, no one knew how, to amass the support needed to take on the formidable outgoing deputy and who claimed that he would regulate the work hours and salaries of plantation workers and establish a great many other regrettable measures in the name of some vague principles of equity and humanism. Aside from his harebrained schemes, Larue's complexion was not absolutely white, which to La Tour-Major added insult to injury. It was natural then for this fascinating political joust to displace in his guests' concerns the mood swings of a temperamental mountain.

"With a little luck, those half-savages will think the mountain is angry and they'll be too busy trying to pacify it with the help of God knows what sacrifices to even consider going to vote," observed Larrivée coldly.

That idea seemed to gladden everyone.

"Basically, these minor eruptions are a very good thing," concluded La Chevrotière, who wanted one last swig of Armagnac, but noticed too late that his glass was empty and took instead a gulp of air which made him cough a little.

BAPTISTE'S ESCAPADES WERE DISCOVERED WHEN he was caught slipping back between the bars of his cell at dawn on his fifth day of captivity. Not sure if he should be punished for his repeated escapes from prison or for having, so to speak, broken his way in, officials decided to treat him with redoubled severity, and the prisoner was moved to a far less comfortable jail, one from which there was no way to escape.

The dungeon was stifling, as if all the air had been withdrawn. Unpleasant condensation dripped off the half-metre thick walls, which were marked in places by a sticky, greenish goo that could have been the blood of the stones, flowing since the dawn of time in the silence and the dim light. Over the years the mortar had been covered with a kind of silvery lichen, rough to the touch, that seemed to be half-plant, half-mineral.

When he first saw this new prison, Baptiste could only think of a tomb. The bulky stone structure was topped with a vaulted roof; its crude ventilation hole, along with a tiny window, constituted the only opening aside from a door with a hatch in it. A small bright circle moved slowly across the ground, following the angle of the sun, a kind of sundial in negative, the blade of light indicating the hour of day on a shadowy surface. To learn how much time had elapsed he could also count on the cathedral bells of Notre-Dame de Bon-Port that slowly sounded the twelve strokes of noon, later on the angelus and vespers. No other sound passed through the thick walls, and soon the prisoner was grateful for the metallic rustling of the feet and antennae of the cockroaches that shared his cell, without whose ceaseless swarming he would have feared he'd gone deaf. For the first time in his life he did not hear the familiar breathing of the sea. The world no longer existed.

Baptiste thought he was still asleep but was already nearly awake, waving his hands in front of his face, trying in vain to brush away a swarm of buzzing flies and to dispel the acrid stench that caught at his throat. The all too familiar smell had followed him throughout his childhood, when he shared a straw mattress with the youngest of his cousins, Siméon, who wet their bed every night, a smell that soaked his too-short trousers, his well-worn shirts, his too-frizzy hair. Of the whole family, no one had hair as bushy, as finely frizzy, or skin as black.

His uncle and his aunt were decent folk who dis-
charged their Christian duty in exemplary fashion, looking after this child who wasn't theirs, giving him food and
lodging and asking in return only that, instead of going to
school like other boys his age, he spend his days on the
beach, gathering mollusks and shellfish from which his
aunt would make the soups she sold at the market. The
last piece of meat or fish at the very bottom of the pot, the
smallest and stringiest, was always reserved for him. He
was allowed to sit at the table to eat after all the others
had finished their meal. And his aunt made sure she gave
Raoul's clothes to Baptiste once they were threadbare,
when it would have been so easy to throw them out.
Sometimes at nightfall he was even allowed to try to
decipher a few lines in the textbooks of his cousins, who
burst out laughing at his hesitations, while every Sunday
they lent him a pair of shoes to wear to church where he
could not, however, sit with the rest of the family as the
pew was not big enough, and had to stand at the back of
the nave. Decent folk, indeed.

Preferring to spend his time on the street rather than
with his aunt and uncle, often only coming home for
supper, Baptiste had learned the labyrinthine lanes of
Saint-Pierre so well that he could have found his way
blindfolded. He could pilfer a ripe papaya or a fragrant

piece of cheese from a stall whenever the urge struck him, sure that the wronged merchant could never catch him in the maze of winding streets that lacked both traffic signs and official names but were designated by colourful nicknames: Duel Alley, Stairway to Heaven, Road to Hell – the last two famous for their brothels.

As no one was concerned about his comings and goings, he liked to stroll around the port, where a gaudy crowd milled about, made up of sailors, their hides tanned by salt and sun; girls whose long lace petticoats showed under their slightly too-short skirts, giving people a view of little pointed boots splotched with mud; stray dogs; merchants jabbering a mixture of languages. Of these, Baptiste had learned enough to designate in more than a dozen patois, pidgins, and Creoles, certain essential notions which transcended borders and cultures: *sea, eat, money, rum.*

Songs and pieces of music rose up from the boats from Europe and the Americas that were moored at the long wooden jetties. Baptiste had gradually learned to identify the accents, just as he could tell from inhaling the aromas that came from their holds if the boats were transporting spices, fabrics, or slaves, a trade that – outlawed fifty years earlier – was nonetheless still flourishing. Without ever needing to be warned, he steered cautiously clear of those.

· · · · · · · ·

Baptiste opened his eyes at the break of dawn. A slight breeze was coming in the tiny window. He unfolded his aching legs, got up and, with a few steps, crossed the dungeon, shoulders stooped, head down, like a man who has lost something. The silence seemed even deeper than in the dark of night, and he tried to whistle two or three notes simply to hear any sound beside that of his own breathing and his feet on the ground, but his lips were too dry. The jug of water brought to him the day before was nearly empty. He took a cautious sip, not knowing when it would be refilled or replaced, and for a second he wondered if he'd simply been left there to die. Automatically, he slipped his hand into his pocket but his fingers touched only fabric so thin it was frayed. He lay down and curled up in the middle of the cell, directly under the opening, from where he could spy a patch of grey sky turning pink, humming quietly a tune the coffee pickers sang to cheer themselves up in the midday sun.

"I HAVE COM . . ." BEGAN MONSIEUR DE LA Chevrotière, who came to a halt like a statue, puffed out his chest and produced a fantastic sneeze, after which he began again, ever so faintly tearful: "I have complete confidence," brandishing the study prepared by the "scientific commission" set up specifically to scale Mount Pelée, see what was going on there and write a report that would calm troubled minds – and at the same time confirm that an election would be held despite a persistent rumour that it would be put off until a date as yet undetermined.

For more than a week now a very pale grey ash had been falling onto the city, bleaching roads, houses, even passersby who hadn't thought to take an umbrella or a parasol. In Martinique, for the first time in centuries, there were no longer Blacks or Whites, all being covered with a fine powder such as duchesses and courtesans used to sprinkle on their faces and their wigs.

The inhabitants of the small villages scattered at the foot of Mount Pelée were flocking into town, sure they would be safe there. The water in the cascade rushing down the mountainside was now as grey and dense as molten lead; the animals that drank there were afflicted with horrible diarrhea and when it was over they would sometimes lie on their sides and never get up again. Before long the dust falling from the sky covered them, turning them into statues of horses, goats, and dogs.

The gentlemen from the scientific commission, at that moment sitting with the cream of the island's bourgeoisie and sipping cool white wine, hadn't exactly climbed to the mountain top, having been stopped along the way by toxic vapours from the vents, bothered by the sweltering heat that soaked Mount Pelée, their progress hampered by streams of steaming mud, combined obstacles any one of which would have been enough to make them turn on their heels which, incidentally, were shod in kidskin boots. They had not thought it necessary to inform La Tour-Major of this detail, but had they done so it wouldn't have changed anything. As they had written in the report now being passed from hand to hand they had been able to observe:

1. That none of the phenomena to date were in the least abnormal but, on the contrary, were identical to the phenomena observed in every other volcano;

2. That the volcanic craters being for the most part open, the vapours and mud would continue to expand, as had already happened, without provoking earthquakes or ejections of eruptive rocks;

3. That the numerous detonations frequently heard were caused by explosions of vapours in the chimney and not at all by a collapse of the terrain;

4. That the streams of mud and hot water were confined to the valley of the Blanche River;

5. That the relative positions of the craters and valleys running to the sea indicated that Saint-Pierre was absolutely secure;

6. That the blackish waters flowing in the Des Pères, Basse-Pointe, Prêcheur, and other rivers had preserved their ordinary temperature and owed their abnormal colour to the ashes they carried.

The result, they declared, was that "Mount Pelée was no more dangerous to Saint-Pierre than Vesuvius was to Naples."

Magnanimously, the members of the commission guaranteed that they would continue to follow the situation – from a reasonable distance – and to keep the population informed.

"Not at all worried," concluded Monsieur de La Chevrotière.

THE WALLS OF THE DUNGEON WERE COVERED with graffiti left over the years by other prisoners. Some, drawn with a piece of charred wood or a pebble, were nearly erased; others had been carved into the stone where Baptiste could decipher the marks by running his finger over them the way he'd once seen a blind man read a book. There were names of men who might now be alive or dead, dates that corresponded to nothing, small obscene drawings, flowers, birds. His favourite was a hollowed-out circle with lines of different lengths radiating from it. He didn't know if the aim had been to draw a sun or a star, but several times a day he would trace the curve of the minute celestial body embedded in the damp stone.

As a child he would sometimes kneel to draw in the sand pictures that the sea would erase almost immediately. More than anything else, he loved the long hours spent not far from town alone on the beaches, some as black as soot and scattered with grains of silver like stars in an inky sky, while others, gold like ripe fruit, unfurled their blondness in the sunshine. He would catch sharp-clawed violet crabs with one brisk movement as they scurried diagonally on their oddly articulated claws; dig with his toe when he saw small bubbles forming on the surface of the sand, announcing the presence of a clam; fill baskets with crustaceans and conches for his aunt to make the spicy soup she would announce loudly and sell to passersby. When no one was looking, he would gulp the pink or grey contents of a shell.

He would stick his head underwater and for a few minutes the world ceased to exist, replaced by that other bluish universe where he was weightless, as if he'd been set free. His fluid movements would encounter a resistance that could have been due to the silence they had to pass through – the pirouettes of fish fleeing at his approach; the slow flight of the enormous ray, nearly invisible against the sand, half-bird, half-fish; the hypnotic sway of water weeds like long hair blown by the wind; the erratic leaps of scallops advancing in short bursts – all bathed in a similar weightlessness where time itself seemed suspended.

Now and then a wave deeper than others would grab him and he would let himself swirl as if in a sandstorm, not knowing where the surface was and where the depths, rolling with the water until it calmed down and dropped him peacefully on the beach. From those dives he would bring back a pearly nautilus, a tiny sea horse, or a red starfish, which he would return to the sea a few hours later, humble gifts from the ocean, all of them treasures.

One day when he was around ten years old, he had opened an oyster to discover, nestled against the soft and fleshy creature in the shell, a pearl the size of his fingernail, not perfectly spherical, its whiteness reflecting all the colours of the rainbow, like a minuscule, nearly full moon fallen into the sea and swallowed whole by a greedy mollusk.

"What did you find?" his cousin Raoul had shouted when he saw him absorbed in something taken out of the foam at his feet.

Without thinking, Baptiste had thrown back his head and gulped the slippery, salty oyster.

"Nothing," he replied, displaying the empty shell.

Not until Raoul had turned his back and resumed his own explorations did Baptiste spit the pearl into his hand, then slip it into his trouser pocket, wondering if he had just stolen something, though he'd have had trouble saying from whom. But he knew that when the moment came he would have to confess this wicked deed to God.

On the first Tuesday of every month he went to confession with his cousins, waiting his turn in the dim nave under the threatening gaze of the statues of saints, some of which shed scented wax tears once a year. Sitting on the hard seat in the confessional, he observed through the fine lattice work the glistening eye of the priest to whom he said: "Bless me, Father, for I have sinned." Next came a list of his misdeeds in recent weeks which he strove scrupulously to report in order, in case that made any difference. The priest reminded him every time that the least of his offences added another thorn to Christ's crown and imposed Hail Marys and Our Fathers in proportion to the number and gravity of his sins: two Our Fathers for stealing a coconut, three for a papaya. Over time the image of those new thorns driven into the Saviour's flesh became unbearable to Baptiste and at age twelve he decided to avoid all sins, to stop pilfering and to obey his aunt and uncle on all matters. One Tuesday he appeared at confession triumphant, certain that he had not contributed at all to the suffering of Our Lord, impatient to tell his feat to the priest, who would be sure to congratulate him. He pulled the velvet curtain in the confessional behind him and silently took a seat. He wasn't sure how to begin. On the other side of the finely worked grille he could make out the face of the priest in silhouette. The smell of incense, beeswax, and garlic floated in the air.

"Well?" asked the priest after a moment.

"Hello, Father," replied Baptiste, his voice quavering

slightly from combined fear and pride. "This month I didn't sin."

The face turned towards him, a grey mask whose features were erased by the dimness.

"No sins. Whoever heard of such a thing? Presumption, my child, is a wicked fault," said the priest.

Baptiste didn't get the connection so he waited, hands clasped, for the *curé* to go on.

"So you've done nothing wrong, you haven't stolen, you haven't fought . . ."

"No, Father."

"Maybe you've disobeyed your mother or father?"

Baptiste wanted to point out how impossible the latter hypothesis would have been but he decided not to and merely replied:

"No, Father."

He now could detect a hint of impatience in the voice of the *curé*, who went on:

"Lied then?"

"No, Father, I haven't told a lie."

"Not even by omission?"

Baptiste didn't know what the *curé* meant by that and not daring to ask, said again, but less certainly:

"No, Father."

Sensing he was on to something, Father Blanchot leaned forward and whispered:

"But you've committed impure deeds or had impure thoughts, haven't you?"

The smell of garlic was stronger now. Baptiste didn't know what the *curé* meant by that either. His confessions had never gone on so long: usually, he would admit that he'd filched a mango and gone for a stroll after nightfall when his aunt had forbidden it, the *curé* would absent-mindedly impose a penance, and that was it until the following month. Now he almost wished he had a crime to acknowledge.

"I don't know, Father."

"Aha!" said the priest smugly, leaning back comfortably. "Girls?"

Of course Baptiste liked looking at girls and he would sometimes drop a coin so he would have to bend down and could look under their skirts. But that could not be a sin.

As Baptiste wasn't replying, the *curé* suggested, his voice even lower:

"Boys?"

The only boys he rubbed shoulders with were his cousins and even if he hoped every morning on waking up that Siméon would stop wetting the bed, he was fairly sure that wasn't what the *curé* meant.

"No, Father," he declared.

The confessor heaved a sigh, brought his face close to the grille again so Baptiste could see his nose, his chin, and his eyebrows cut into little squares, and declared: "There are many things that wound Our Lord, but of all the sins, lying is the most loathsome. To shed the urge to tell falsehoods, young man, do ten Stations of the Cross, recite fifty Our Fathers and ten Hail Marys. And come back when you're ready to confess the wrongs that taint your soul."

The small partition separating the confessional slammed shut and for a long moment, Baptiste sat unmoving in the dark. The following month and every other month until he turned sixteen, when once and for all he stopped begging Father Blanchot for mercy, he invented a list of misdeeds that he left at the *curé's* feet as a rotten offering, then went away whistling a tune – after spitting in the holy water stoup.

In his cell that night, when there was utter darkness around him, Baptiste dug in the beaten earth floor until he found a pebble sufficiently sharp and pointed, and he began to trace around the circle engraved in the stone a broad rectangle divided into squares. Behind it he scrawled waves, sand, and some fluffy clouds. Then he lay down in the dark again, looking towards the invisible wall where he had opened a window.

THE NAUSEATING SMELL THAT PELÉE SOMETIMES gave off for days, a sulphur stench amusingly called "mountain farts," had been bathing the city for weeks, forcing the populace to keep their windows sealed tight despite the heat. The lovelies on the streets untied their long scarves and placed them over their noses and mouths, making them look a little like the veiled women of the desert, the difference being that the multicoloured fabrics in which they wrapped themselves teemed with flowers, birds, and vegetation, and that they didn't hesitate to lift a corner to show off the dazzle of a smile where sometimes a gold tooth shone.

Both household pets and farm animals behaviour began to behave strangely, some refusing to eat while others, who'd always been absolutely gentle, delivered kicks and bites whenever anyone tried to tie them up.

Finally, something new was observed, but for obvious reasons only among the most affluent citizens of Saint-Pierre; silver objects were covered overnight with a dark coating similar to charcoal.

Father Blanchot, summoned before lauds while eating his morning boiled egg, thought at first that it was a bad joke.

"What's the matter?" he snapped at a trembling altar boy. It was common knowledge that the *curé* disliked being disturbed during meals, which he ate alone and in silence. Madame Pinson, his housekeeper, put on felt slippers to serve and to clear the table.

"Father," stammered the boy, twisting a corner of his child's size soutane, "it's the ciborium . . ."

"The ciborium? What on earth have you done to it? You can't have broken it, it's sterling silver! Or else . . . have you lost it, you little devil?" he roared, brandishing a toast finger like a threat.

"No, Father, nothing like that . . . But . . . it's all black."

"Don't talk nonsense, lad," said the *curé*, reassured in spite of everything, taking a sip of *café au lait*. "You forgot to shine it for a few days, you were too busy playing, and now it's slightly tarnished. Don't waste any more time, go and polish it before the service!"

He tried to brush the intruder away with the back of his hand but the child refused to vanish.

"I mean, Father, it's not just the ciborium, it's also the chalice, the monstrance . . ."

"What are you talking about, you disrespectful boy?"

"And the candlesticks, Father."

Father Blanchot got up grudgingly and, glancing at his still half-full plate, warned:

"Watch out if you're fooling around, young man."

But the altar boy wasn't fooling around.

The good Father had never done so well since his arrival in Saint-Pierre. His church was always full; at certain hours the faithful who had been unable to find a seat inside crowded together out front all the way to the steps and listened from there to the sermon that came to them through the half-open doors, which let into the nave a fine black dust smelling of sulphur.

For a variety of reasons that he couldn't fully explain, Father Blanchot had always harboured a fascination with the Apocalypse of Saint John. Certainly he appreciated the more subtle rhetorical devices set forth in the Book of Job or in Ecclesiastes, among others. But this fat and rather pusillanimous man, who liked his comfort and his own habits and customs, experienced at the mere mention of lion-headed horses, poisoned grasshoppers, and other baleful harbingers of Revelation, a shudder such as he hadn't felt since his teenage years, when watching one of his classmates with flowing blond hair being thrashed by a teacher who always had a long wooden ruler tucked into the waist of his soutane. Yes, definitely, the subject inspired him. There was matter there for more than one edifying sermon.

He had long lamented the fact that it was so hard to waken his flock to the threat of torture awaiting those who did not obey the precepts of Our Lord during their earthly existence. This did not prevent him from brandishing the terrifying promise of eternal fire and damnation every week before parishioners already half stunned by the heat, fanning themselves by waving their Bibles in front of their faces as if trying to chase away a fly.

All that had changed around a month earlier. At the first indistinct rumbling of Mount Pelée, tearful women had banged on the closed doors of the cathedral in the light of a mauve dawn to confess sins they had just most willingly committed. Those who had led them onto this ruinous way – or who'd followed them, it varied – were quick to copy them and soon the House of God was filled night and day, ringing out at all hours with the *curé*'s powerful voice recalling the tragic destinies of vile Sodom and Gomorrah, of impure Babylon, of arrogant Babel. Morning, noon, and evening, the altar boys polished the liturgical vessels, which turned black almost before their eyes. The housekeeper had been pressed into service and was watching over the preparation of enough communion wafers in the presbytery kitchen to feed all those starving souls who by the grace of God would be satisfied.

Writing sermons had never been so easy for Father Blanchot: he just had to look out the window to see what new scourge was raging and, inevitably, the Bible would offer him an illustration or a dreadful explanation. Should smoke rise from the crater in the morning, he would announce in a lugubrious voice: "There arose a smoke out of the pit, as the smoke of a great furnace; and the sun and the air were darkened by reason of the smoke of the pit." Should the flagstone floor tremble beneath the feet of the islanders gathered in the church, he would go on in a voice like thunder: "I beheld when he opened the sixth seal, and lo, there was a great earthquake; and the sun became black as sackcloth of hair, and the moon became as blood; and the stars of heaven fell unto the earth, even as a fig tree casteth her untimely figs, when she is shaken of a mighty wind." Of course no one had yet seen stars crash to earth, but the mountain spat flying sparks into the night, sending down a disturbing extravaganza of yellow, red, and orange against the blackness of the sky, and at dawn the *curé* trumpeted: "And there followed hail and fire mingled with blood, and they were cast upon the earth; and a third of the earth was burned up and a third of the trees was burned up, and all green grass was burned up."

But what was most spectacular in his sermon, what he was most proud of, came to him in the form of a swarming mass, a veritable rain of insects beating down on the town. Creatures never before in human memory seen in broad daylight – hairy spiders that lived in burrows, eyeing their prey; red scorpions; foot-long millipedes that didn't hesitate to attack the hens – and others they knew all too well: fearsome carpenter ants, green grasshoppers with legs like twigs, innumerable cockroaches, all came down the mountain slopes to storm the streets of Saint-Pierre.

Hordes of bats emerged from the darkness of caves at midday to flutter, blind, above the heads of the terrified islanders, sometimes brushing close enough to lift a lock of hair with their crooked fingers.

Overnight, alleys were teeming with snakes that slipped into the slightest chink between the boards or the stones of houses; and the inhabitants found them in their kitchens, their bathtubs, even between their sheets. People now walked with eyes to the ground, while in the sky the crater kept spitting grey clouds and orange flames. Some talked of seeing hideous reptiles crawl, undulating, into the sea and disappear into the waves; others even swore that snakes had been found coiled up in the holds of ships, hidden among the rigging.

The *curé* had no doubt: it was unquestionably the Apocalypse. He had witnessed it from the outset, following its progress step by step while its spectacle of fire unfolded before his dazzled eyes. God was speaking to him by showing him how to read in the surrounding countryside the mysterious story that had been transcribed into the sacred texts thousands of years before.

The thought filled him with elation when he presented to all, several times a day, the blood of Christ in a chalice that turned black in his hands.

By these three was the third part of men killed, by the fire and by the smoke, and by the brimstone, which issued out of their mouths. And there appeared another wonder in heaven; and behold a great red dragon, having seven heads and ten horns, and seven crowns upon his heads. And his tail drew the third part of the stars of heaven, and did cast them to the earth: and the dragon stood before the woman which was ready to be delivered, for to devour her child as soon as it was born. And I saw three unclean spirits like frogs come out of the mouth of the dragon, and out of the mouth of the beast, and out of the mouth of the false prophet. And after these things I saw another angel come down from heaven, having great power; and the earth was lightened with his glory. And he cried mightily with a strong voice, saying . . .

Here, he had to break off, choking in the acrid smell filling the church. The crater spewing flames was trying to prevent him from spreading the Good Word – ah! He would rise up, alone, before the diabolical mountain. He coughed, tried to get his breath back, choked again, finally reached out mechanically for the cup resting nearby on the altar. He gulped some wine and felt better.

Babylon the great is fallen, is fallen . . . he repeated, startling certain members of the congregation, some of whom, knowing little of the cursed city's history, searched briefly with their eyes for a woman called Babylon who had stumbled in the aisle. *And is become the habitation of devils, and the hold of every foul sprit, and a cage of every unclean and hateful bird. For all nations have drunk of the wine of the wrath of her fornication, and the kings of the earth are waxed rich through the abundance of her delicacies. And I heard another voice from heaven, saying, Come out of her, my people, that ye be not partakers of her sins, and that ye receive not of her plagues. For her sins have reached unto heaven, and God hath remembered her iniquities. Standing afar off for the fear of her torment, saying, Alas, alas that great city Babylon, that mighty city! For in one hour is thy judgment come. And the merchants of the earth shall weep and mourn over her; for no man buys their merchandise anymore: The merchandise of gold, and silver, and precious stones, and of pearls, and fine linen, and purple, and silk, and scarlet, and all thy fine wood, and all manner vessels of ivory, and all manner vessels of most precious woods, and of brass, and iron, and marble, And cinnamon, and odours and ointments, and frankincense, and wine, and oil, and fine flour, and wheat, and beasts, and sheep, and horses, and chariots, and slaves, and souls of men.*

These sombre words, ringing out like the trumpets of Judgment Day in the dimness of the nave, were followed by a silence so deep that one could hear the wheezing of the stunned parishioners on the long wooden pews. They held their Bibles motionless at the level of their chests, a frail paper rampart against the firestorm that threatened at any moment to swoop down on them, uncertain if it was the fruit of divine rage or of the malice of the devil.

THE HATCH IN THE BOTTOM OF THE HEAVY
wooden door creaked open, a heel of bread was tossed
inside, and a hand reached out for the empty jug Baptiste
was supposed to give over promptly. With any luck it
would be returned a few hours later, filled with tepid
water. He hurried, knowing they had a brief attention
span. The night before he had taken too long to emerge
from the sound sleep he'd fallen into abruptly, as though
he'd fainted, and the hatch had slammed shut before he
could hold out the nearly empty jug. This time, he managed to hand over the receptacle, which disappeared
straightaway.

Sitting on the ground opposite the window he'd
drawn on the blank wall, he sucked on the hard chunk of
bread. He softened it under his tongue, revealing the
abrasive texture of the coarsely ground wheat and corn.
When the crumb had regained a little of its elasticity he
chewed slowly, waiting for its taste to spread before he
tore off a new mouthful.

Long hours went by, maybe the whole day, before he heard again the click of the key in the lock that announced the hatch was about to be opened. With one leap he was at the door, holding out his hand for the jug, which was released before he had time to close his fingers on the rounded neck or to grab a handle. The precious liquid spilled onto the ground, which drank it up at once. The hatch was shut and Baptiste dropped to all fours like a dog and tried to lap up what was left, but the earth had swallowed it all. He stood and looked at the dark spot, its outlines already blurred. Tears of helplessness were already filling his eyes; he swallowed them. They too would have been wasted water.

· · · · · · · ·

Meanwhile, *L'Opinion* was trying to reassure the population by calling on history:

We have read the report addressed to the Governor in 1851, by the Commission which had studied the volcano. The result was that the eruption of the mountain does not represent any danger. This volcano has released nothing save mud and ashes. Inhabitants of this island, sleep well, dear friends!

Les Colonies, whose editor-in-chief was a friend of La Tour-Major and one of his most ardent supporters, was doing the same, reporting on any "oddities" that affected the island, but careful to put together articles, advertisements, and commentaries at the back of the journal that demonstrated that life on the island was following its course and there was no cause for alarm.

On May 2 he published a notice stating that the grand excursion organized by the gymnastics and firing club, planned to close with a picnic on the summit of Mount Pelée, would be held as announced, on Sunday the fourth. Weather permitting, the participants would spend the day creating happy memories they would cherish for a long time. If they had climbed the mountain that Sunday afternoon and been able to pierce the fog with their rifles, or if some practice of gymnastics had let them rise above the strip of poisoned clouds that encircled its upper third, club members would have seen a smooth sea, coal-grey, on which floated hundreds of dead birds in lugubrious black-and-white clusters. But no one ventured onto the mountain that day and even at *Les Colonies* they had to resign themselves, on the eve of the celebrations, to publishing the following laconic notice in the midst of the obituaries: *The outing planned for tomorrow will not take place, as the crater is absolutely inaccessible.*

· · · · · · · ·

"You see, my dear, I told them," began Monsieur de La Chevrotière, turning towards his wife who rolled her eyes, unseen, because the darkness was total, "it would be best to avoid panic and to do so, nothing could compare with organized entertainments." For several hours now, he had been giving her a detailed account of the meeting held earlier that evening, when the La Tour-Major clan had decided on the strategy to adopt so as not to let the election get away from them. She had thought she could put an end to the wave of words by getting into bed, but her husband continued to hold forth while donning pyjamas and nightcap and, lying comfortably beside her, back propped against two down-filled pillows, he continued his soliloquy: "Enough modesty, they had no choice but to recognize that I had the best idea. And I—" Just then he was interrupted by a small piece of plaster that fell from the ceiling and landed on his cheek.

A few seconds later, the entire dwelling folded like a house of cards collapsing inwards. A cloud of poisoned gas had gushed down the mountain to drown the city, while at the summit, in the purple darkness, white flashes of lightning shot through the sky.

"I . . . I am . . . dying," Monsieur de La Chevrotière managed to get out finally, and his wife, with a superhuman effort, covered her ears with her hands.

AT FOUR A.M. ON THAT ASCENSION DAY, MAY 8,
1902, a man leaning on the bar of the Blessé-Bobo went
to look at his watch and realized it had been stolen; a
woman unable to sleep was getting up to gaze out the
window to see if the white soot falling from the sky for
days had finally stopped; two lovers met at the Agnes
Fountain as they did every night, and left together, impatient; a dog dreamed that he was chasing a cat, his chops
and whiskers quivering as he uttered shrill little cries in
his sleep; an old man on his deathbed suddenly felt better
and found the courage to haul himself up on his pillows
and ask the servant dozing in a chair beside his bed, cap
askew, for a drink; the Sun was still on the other side of
Earth; the murmuring wind was tickling the palm fronds;
a gendarme was writing a report and drinking black
coffee; a prostitute on her stool, lipstick more or less
intact, was waiting, staring vacantly, for dawn to come at
last; a butler above all suspicion was stuffing silver spoons
into a bag, intending to sell them the next morning; a

child was waking from one nightmare only to fall into another; the sea was leaving on the sand handfuls of shells, tangled tufts of seaweed, and pieces of driftwood licked clean until they were white and smooth as bone; a mother exhausted from sitting up with her sick son laid her head on the pillow next to the child's clammy head; a horse in a stable fell to his knees, then collapsed; a hen nearby laid an egg then stared at it, dumbfounded; a poet peered in vain at the smudged sky, awaiting inspiration, and without realizing it, left an ink spot where he'd intended to begin a sonnet; moths in the hundreds scorched their wings on streetlamp bulbs; a lover slipped in silence into his mistress's bed while her husband slept some rooms away, and put his hand on her breast, half-smiling; spread-eagled on the dirt floor of his cell, Baptiste listened to the swarm of cockroaches; a sailor on a ship moored in the harbour leaned over the ship's rail to vomit a bitter mixture of rum and ale; at the bottom of the sea a telegraph cable broke; bats flew back to the caves where they spent the daylight hours hanging by their feet; the pressman at *L'Opinion* watched the metal monster spit out long rolls of paper; Gontran de La Chevrotière farted in his sleep and was deeply satisfied; a colony of termites completed a castle of earth and saliva as tall as a man; Father Blanchot dreamed about a beast with seven heads, all blond, that looked at him with blue eyes; a former slave put her hand unconsciously on her ankle where there used to be fetters; an ancient banana tree in the depths of the forest fell amid a rustling of leaves heard by no one; under its warm crust, the earth seethed; in a hospital bed, a man who'd been told he would never walk again was running in his dream, while one floor higher a white woman gave birth to a black baby; a pickpocket examining the night's spoils admired a gold watch whose second hand was moving by fits and starts.

And then, in a moment, all that was blown away, and infinitely more; all multiplied by a hundred, a thousand, thirty thousand: wiped out.

For a few hours now the atmosphere in the solitary dungeon in the prison yard has been saturated with very fine coal-black dust that comes in through the slightest crack and hangs in the air like sand in water. Baptiste's gullet is on fire, his eyes dry and sore, face and hands flayed like wounds rubbed with salt. He could swear that it has been days since he's been given anything to drink, although his prison is sunk into a false darkness that makes the day look very much like the night.

The distant rumbling that has not been silent for a week and has become so familiar it has become a new kind of silence, all at once seems to explode. A blast shakes the stone walls and even the ground where Baptiste is lying. A few seconds later, the room is filled with an even denser cloud smelling of sulphur, which catches at his throat and keeps him from breathing. He takes off his tattered vest and ties it around his head. With the fabric covering his nose and mouth, he manages to take short breaths. With cautious steps he approaches the tiny window and jumps up with all his strength, trying to see outside. He finally is able to clutch the bars, but immediately cries out, gazes at his palms where already blisters filled with brackish water are forming. He cannot give a meaning to the images glimpsed: blackened shapes stretched out or standing; trees with leaves of fire; apocalyptic visions that he persuades himself are the fruit of his imagination, thrown into turmoil by thirst and fear. The air becomes more and more rare inside the stone walls, which are as hot to the touch as his burning forehead. He tries in vain to get away from the source of the danger by curling up in a corner of the room, hugging his legs with his arms and trembling. He senses that death is near, that it might already be there.

Then, without wanting to, almost as if he were looking from a distance at the actions of a man who looks like him, he realizes that he is taking off his pants, which he observes for a moment before urinating on them. The cloudy stream appears to be as viscous as the unbreathable air that fills the dungeon. This strange man with his own features takes the soaking trousers and fits them as best he can between the bars of the window to keep the smoke and dust from getting in. Baptiste follows his movements, vaguely interested, admiring even, as if the stranger were more and more alien to him. Then he drops his head and closes his eyes.

—

Behind his eyelids dances the sea that was always the same and every day different. Sometimes swollen by storms, its waves like shifting mountains hemmed with lead-coloured foam; at other times slack and smooth as a sheet of ice, its surface pierced now and then by a seabird diving head first, wings folded, then reappearing with a wriggling fish in its beak, a mirror in which were reflected motionless inverted ships, sails furled, masts pointed towards the centre of the earth; shimmering green and blue, like the feathers of some wild parrot that must be approached with great care. At certain hours, before a storm, it became drained of all colour and all substance until it was no more than a shadow sea, its yellowish glimmers reminiscent of the overripe flesh of mangoes. On those days more than others, he couldn't tell whether the clouds were lending their colour to the ocean or the water was dictating its mood to the sky, the grey of both merging to draw a horizon that seemed to unite, not separate them. Then that line disappeared as well and there was no longer anything in him or around him but fog.

When he opens his eyes a few hours later, he knows in a flash that the end of the world has come and that he has been forgotten.

When he was half-dragged, half-carried from the dungeon that had nearly been his tomb, Baptiste, dazzled, had to protect his eyes from the overly bright light assaulting him. The landscape revealed itself little by little, outlines blurred and hazy at first, then more and more precise – unbearable.

It was not an apocalyptic landscape he was crossing but the landscape of the day after the apocalypse, once the destruction has been accomplished. Of the houses, streets, city that he'd known there remained nothing but heaps of rubble and ash pierced by charred beams like grim gallows. One half of a miraculously preserved sign, of which the other part had been blown away by the blast of the volcano, announced, incomprehensible and pathetic:

HÔ   CAR   E

Smoke was rising everywhere from the ruins carrying with it an indescribable stench. The odour of scorched wood could not entirely mask the smell of sulphur, which was in turn dominated by a third, repulsive smell, that of burned flesh.

Baptiste choked, coughed, tried to say: "Take me back inside," but was only able to produce a series of guttural sounds that could have expressed pain as much as gratitude.

"Sssh," advised one of the men holding him by the elbow, "don't try to talk. You had an amazing stroke of luck, do you know that? We've been looking for three days and you're the first we've found."

"Th-the first prisoner?" Baptiste managed to ask, almost inaudibly.

There was a moment when the two men flanking him exchanged a look but said nothing. Then the taller replied:

"No. The first and only one in town."

A NURSE CAME MORNING AND NIGHT TO CHANGE
his dressings, give him something to drink, and feed him,
like a bird, a few mouthfuls of puréed fruit that he had
trouble swallowing. He felt as if his throat were still con-
stricted by the smoke and the red-hot cinders.

In the darkness he could see dragons spitting fire,
hideous sea serpents snapping up the ships in the depths
of the ocean, so he slept as little as possible and was careful always to have a lamp lit beside him. After some
twenty days he was able to stand up and take a few steps,
leaning on the doctor's arm, then sit for half an hour in
the armchair by the open window and look at the sky, no
longer masked by the crenellated foliage of the palm
trees. Then he started taking short walks alone in the
deserted city and he felt for his massacred, charred, petrified, suppurating island a love such as he had never experienced when it was verdant and sweetly scented.

In some places nothing indicated the presence of
dwellings, shops, or even streets; everywhere the ground

was covered with a thick layer of ill-assorted debris coated with a fine dust in which his feet left a solitary, labyrinthine trail. Unconsciously he bent down now and then to pick up – as he had once picked up shells and agates – a fountain pen monogrammed in gold, a mother-of-pearl button, a marble that in the heat had assumed the shape of a bean.

Absurdly, some papers had survived the holocaust that had turned wood, fabric, even the bricks of the buildings to ashes, and Baptiste was soon sifting through the ruins that on June 15 were still smoking, finding sheets of paper flying in the wind or stuck between a charred shoe and a cash register with its keys welded together. He assembled a bouquet of pages that grew thicker every day. Monsieur Hugo's Cosette and the Thénardier couple rubbed shoulders with a list of vegetable seeds adapted to a tropical climate, followed by a baptismal register written on a larger sheet of the creamy white stationery reserved for the administration, and then, on a page with ragged edges, something in incomprehensible letters that might have been Greek, expenditures for the month of March by the Hôtel Excelsior, and the final pages of the Apocalypse of Saint John, on which could still be read, in small, thick letters: *And whosoever was not found written in the book of life was cast into the lake of fire.*

Leafing through the bundle of papers, some with scorched edges, others a nearly immaculate white, some still bearing the threads of their unstitched binding like the scar from a poorly sutured wound, he felt he was contemplating the history of his island, broken open, interrupted, in its middle, forever incomplete yet over now.

Some men, fewer women, were pacing the rubble in search not of survivors – they knew now that one individual, only one, had made it through the firestorm, and his name was actually becoming famous – but of traces of those they had loved and lost, searching the ruins in the hope of finding a photo, a button, a pipe testifying to the existence of the dead. They ignored one another, sometimes brushed up against each other seemingly unaware, each one carrying on a quest that he knew was hopeless; sad, slow-moving rubbish collectors who seemed like ghosts back from the kingdom of the dead.

Black birds from who knows where were also pecking through the debris with strident cries; searching among the stones and sometimes rising up with a heavy flapping of wings, holding in their beaks some rosy morsel. They were known as birds of misfortune, not because they had announced the calamity – like their more graceful cousins they had deserted Saint-Pierre weeks before the eruption – but because they ate so heartily.

Baptiste's steps brought him back despite himself to the stone dungeon where he had thought he would perish and to which he owed his life. The small structure now stood alone in the middle of a large field of pulverized and blackened rubble. He paced the periphery, eyes to the ground, unable to admit to himself that he was trying to find the pearl from which he hadn't been separated since childhood and that had become his talisman. His memories grew confused and when he tried to sort them out they got away from him, as if he was trying to grasp a mass of spindrift. It seemed to him then that he'd had the pearl with him in the dungeon, but as soon as he tried to clarify that idea – had he at some point slipped it into his shirt pocket or the seam of his trousers, or had he stored it carefully under his tongue as he often did? – a thousand other possibilities came along and blurred it. The pearl had been stolen from him in the communal cell on the night of his arrest several weeks earlier; he had dropped it on the ground in his impatience to escape that last night; or had he, in a moment of panic when he was not entirely master of his movements, buried it in a corner of the dungeon to protect it against whatever might happen to him? How could he find out?

Baptiste began to search in the rubble, in the pebbles, the dusty shreds of fabric and crumbled cobblestones where insects with countless legs and glossy undersides scuttled, seeming to emerge from the depths of the earth. All at once he spotted the iridescent lustre of a rounded white surface. Incredulous, he bent down, picked up the tiny smooth object, and did not realize until he brought it near to his face that he was holding not the lost pearl but a human tooth.

That day he stopped scrutinizing the ground when he was walking and went home keeping his eyes stubbornly raised towards the sky.

It was weeks before Baptiste reached out for the mirror the nurse had offered him every day to see for himself the marks left on his body by Mount Pelée's anger. He discovered then that his eyes weren't entirely black as he'd always been told and had thought he could confirm by looking at his reflection in the translucent surface of a shop window, or when he checked furtively in the silvering of the gilt mirrors in the La Chevrotière villa: in the pupil of his left eye, sparkling like a fragment of star, was a flake the green of the sea on a fine April day.

Though his face had miraculously been spared, his chest and back were now one big scar. He could not have said whether it was a single injury with countless branches or a thousand burns that had joined and crisscrossed, tracing on his abdomen a labyrinth of cracked and blistered flesh. Where there had been smooth black skin, there was now, spread out like some monstrous nest of vipers, a thousand-branched gash that henceforth was part of him and of which each avenue traced by suffering led ineluctably to horror. The anxious nurse at his side half expected that he would drop the mirror as the wounded so often did when they discovered a body foreign to them, but he did nothing of the kind. Baptiste, impassive, studied minutely every square centimetre of the twists and turns of this new landscape carved on him by Mount Pelée's fires as if he were looking for a path.

Often his words had to cross a similar maze; he would hesitate for a long time before speaking and once he'd started, he would interrupt himself midway, knowing what he was about to say but unable to say it, as if the refractory word, endowed suddenly with a will of its own, were scoffing at him just beyond his reach. The slightest thing distracted him – a falling leaf, a singing bird – and he was filled with a kind of stupefaction that made him stop what he was doing. It seemed that after contemplating the world with the certainty of never seeing it again, he was now condemned to rediscover every fragment of it with the boundless, nearly painful amazement of a first time eternally started afresh.

He was sitting one evening, motionless, looking out to sea, when a man in a suit and patent leather shoes, carrying a bowler hat, silently approached him in the sand.

Darkness was taking over the beach; it seemed to be rising up from the island and into the sky where purple, crimson and charcoal-grey veils pierced with scarlet were dancing. The man came up behind him and inquired:

"Are you Baptiste Cyparis?"

It was the name he'd given to his rescuers and he hadn't felt a need to change it.

"Y-yes."

"The Baptiste Cyparis who survived the eruption of Mount Pelée?"

Still looking out to sea, Baptiste confirmed: "I'm the only one," without specifying whether he meant the only one with the name or that no other man had emerged unscathed from the disaster.

The new arrival held out a visiting card and Baptiste examined it with some surprise. Realizing that Baptiste might not be able to read, the man introduced himself, smiling broadly as if he were announcing some good news:

"My name is Richard Rochester. I am the first recruiting officer for Mister James Bailey, of whom you have undoubtedly heard."

Baptiste just stared at him in an oddly empty way.

"Mr. Bailey runs a circus, the Barnum & Bailey," he went on, "the biggest one in the world, and the most famous. And he would like you to be part of it."

"A circus?" Baptiste repeated.

Determined not to make any assumptions, Rochester began patiently to explain:

"A travelling exhibition as well as a show, under a big top, where people come to admire natural wonders, phenomena, and marvels: a man so strong he can twist steel; a woman so heavy that four men can't to lift her; twins welded together; a bearded lady; horses that can add and subtract; a two-headed sheep—"

"I'm very fond of animals," Baptiste interrupted, as if he had just realized it now. "Maybe I could look after the horses . . ."

"No, that's not what Mr. Bailey had in mind . . ."

"Well, then," he suggested, feeling his chin, "a bearded man?"

Rochester seemed to hesitate between laughter and incredulity.

"No, nothing like that. You. Just you: Baptiste Cyparis, the Man who Survived the Eruption of Pelée Mountain. The Man who Lived through Doomsday."

"B-but," Baptiste stammered, "I'm not like your strongman or your horses . . . I . . . I don't know how to do anything," he confessed.

"Doesn't matter," said the other man. "Let us worry about that."

"But . . . Do you think that people will come just to see me?"

"Trust me, they'll come."

Baptiste replied in a low voice, struggling to get the words out:

"All . . . All right." As Rochester walked away, he stayed there gazing at the sky. All that could now be seen was a thin red strip glowing above the waves.

For long journeys, the circus had a specially outfitted train where acrobats, animal tamers, and phenomena each had their own car, as did the lions, the horses, and even the few aquatic animals that were transported in tanks. For shorter trips, however, they would still form a caravan of dozens of trailers crisscrossing the roads of the United States of America.

The trailer assigned to Baptiste was hardly bigger than the dungeon where he had spent those twenty days that had felt like a century and, like the stone prison, it had a curved vaulted ceiling. At the back was a narrow berth; the centre of the space was occupied by a small, one-legged table fastened to the wall, with an upright chair on either side, all resting on a carpet showing signs of wear. On the opposite wall, next to a faded postcard of the Bay of Naples, stood a shallow cupboard where he discovered, left behind by the previous occupant, a shard of blue-and-white porcelain and a copper ball the size of a quail's egg, amazingly heavy, that he dropped into his pocket before hanging his only clean shirt and trousers in the wardrobe.

On the first night, despite the coolness he lay down on top of the covers, put his head on the pillow, and looked up at the curved ceiling. The roof seemed to be descending slowly towards him while the walls were coming closer, pressing so tightly as to keep him from breathing. He sat up, gasping, and went out into the pitch-black night. From some of the trailers he heard laughter. The windows in a few formed luminous rectangles in the dark where now and then a silhouette passed, as in a shadow theatre.

Cries he did not recognize rose in the night, the animals keeping up a mysterious conversation in their cages. In the distance rang the sounds of the hammers, mallets, and saws of people who would work till morning putting up the big top. Baptiste lay down under the trailer, between the two sets of wheels, with only his head sticking out. In the sky so many stars were blinking it seemed as if some bright dust were being blown by a capricious wind. He startled when he caught a glimpse of the moon appearing from behind a cloud: it was not the moon that lay like a cradle in the sky above his island but a new moon standing up straight, like a knife glistening with spectral brightness in the dark.

When he woke in the wan light of dawn, his face was damp. Stretching his numb limbs, he saw that each blade of grass surrounding him was likewise covered with fine droplets. When he stuck out his tongue to catch the dew pearling on his cheek, it tasted of salt.

On the day after Baptiste's arrival, Rochester took him around the tents and trailers to introduce him to their occupants, pointing out, most often needlessly, a talent or a distinctive feature which in certain cases it would have been more tactful not to mention.

At that time of day everyone was washing and getting ready for late afternoon when men, women, and animals would parade through the small town, accompanied by the brass band, to announce the performances and exhibitions to be featured over the next few days. The trailers and tents seemed to have been pitched at random in the enormous field, some in groups of three or four to form a tight circle like the covered wagons of the settlers heading west at the same time, others on their own, backs turned to the rest. To move from one to the other required a thousand detours among posts where clothes were hung to dry, dogs stretched out on the ground, basins full of water, chests, and valises overflowing with costumes worn out from travel.

"This is Ilsa, our bearded lady," announced Rochester, pointing to a woman in her thirties with very gentle eyes, the lower half of her face indeed covered by a curly, silky-looking beard. She was on the steps of a gaily coloured trailer, busy mending something.

The heat was already overwhelming, although the sun was still low in the sky, and a thin vapour seemed to rise from the earth, shimmering in the distance. Ilsa cooled herself by waving a fan painted with birds of paradise.

"And Qiu and Quan, or Quan and Qiu, I never know which is which, but it doesn't really matter because it's unlikely we'll meet one without the other, isn't that so, boys?" Rochester went on, speaking to two Asian men, small in stature, sitting on a bench outside their tent, who had between them two heads and four legs but just two arms and a shared torso. It wasn't clear if they had understood what Rochester had said but each one, with a hesitant smile, waved to Baptiste, who returned their greeting. They stayed like that for a moment, arms raised, each the inverted image of the other.

Rochester had already moved on.

"And here is Jemma," he continued without stopping, half-opening the flap of a tent to show a mass of flesh glistening in the darkness; Baptiste couldn't tell if it was a back or a belly. The mountain straightened up, pivoted painfully (so it was a back, but hunched over, which explained the difficulty) and shot an unkind glance at Baptiste, then asked, as if he couldn't hear:

"And what can this one do?" Without waiting for an answer, she added, in case a doubt persisted: "I don't like that face. Something fishy about it."

"Don't ask what he can do, Jemma, but what he has done. I'll have you know that Baptiste here survived the Apocalypse."

"Is that all?" asked the woman, unimpressed, wiping her damp forehead, then spitting on the ground before resuming the task of putting on her stockings.

The tour continued and Baptiste's uneasiness grew. It seemed to him that whether from interest or perversity, Barnum & Bailey had assembled some monstrous zoo of which, in spite of himself, he was now part. Not knowing how to articulate his distress, he finally asked Rochester:

"Th-the people travelling with the circus . . . Are they all . . . I mean . . ."

"Yes?"

The other man looked at him as if determined to let him get out of it alone. Baptiste repeated: "Are we all . . . m-monsters?"

He thought he saw a flash of pity in the gaze of the manager, who spoke more softly now:

"Mr. Bailey prefers to say *phenomena*, or even *wonders*. One thing is certain, you are all, from the first to the last, absolutely unique. But the circus also uses performers whose talents are less . . . how to put it? . . . less obvious at first sight – and of course animals, which are accommodated elsewhere."

That first morning, Baptiste saw a strongman, an elastic woman, a pair of midgets, a giant, and the skinniest man in the world, all of whom had the same colourless gaze, as if a part of them were worn out from being looked at too much.

As soon as they'd finished visiting the tents that housed the marvels, Baptiste wanted to know where the animals were kept, then went off by himself to meet the enormous hippopotamus, some white Bengal tigers, the lonely giraffe, and the counting horses.

He finally stopped in front of the lion's cage, staring at the occupant who gave him a fraternal and tired look. "*Bonjour*, my name is Baptiste," he said in a low voice. The animal swished the air with his tail and opened his mouth wide to yawn, revealing two impressive, though greyish, rows of teeth. "And mine is Elie," replied the lion politely. Baptiste could not have said what surprised him most: that the animal had spoken or that he'd done so in such a thin little voice.

But from behind the wild creature appeared shortly a little blonde head, which went on: "And that one's Numa. He looks scary, but he's very gentle." As if to contradict him, the animal let out a lengthy growl and shook his rusty mane. Elie went back to brushing the drab coat and the lion creased his eyes and curled his chops in contentment. The boy couldn't have been more than twelve; his movements were confident and precise, his figure slight. As for the lion, he looked shabby; the skin of his elbows was bare, and his coat came away in clumps as the boy brushed him. One eye was festering and from it oozed a greenish, slimy secretion. The animal raised one tremendous paw to rub it, reopening a wound on his brow that looked as though it never had a chance to heal.

"Are you a tamer?" asked Baptiste.

"No," replied Elie, laughing, but clearly flattered to have been taken for one of those broad-shouldered men the slightest crack of whose whip aroused sighs and fluttering eyelashes from the female spectators. "I just brush him and feed him every day. With Josephine and Matilda," he said, pointing at cages farther away; in one could be seen the giraffe's long neck, her small horned head inspecting the landscape, and in the other the grey mass of the hippopotamus.

Elie emerged from the lion's cage so fast that for a moment, Baptiste thought he'd slipped between the bars, but the young lad closed a small door behind him, bolted it carefully, and suggested: "Come here, if you want I'll show you my favourite." He led Baptiste to a tent off to the side, above which had been hung a large white canopy that offered some shade. Nonetheless the heat inside was nearly suffocating; in the dim light a swarm of invisible flies was buzzing, while on the sand floor stood a big metal tank filled with water. They approached it and when Baptiste leaned over, he saw a creature unlike any he had ever seen, scarcely bigger than a woman, its tapering, graceful form ending in a flat tail, its body white as milk. It was looking at him with velvety little eyes set in a round and prettily mustached face. Baptiste, stupefied, held its gaze while it rose slowly to the surface as if to have a better look at him, appearing at once curious and infinitely sad.

"Is . . . is that a mermaid?" he asked.

"A manatee," Elie corrected him.

The manatee's head was now out of the water and in its round eyes Baptiste could see his own trembling silhouette leaning forward.

BAPTISTE RAN INTO THE RENOWNED JAMES BAILEY only once during the time he was with the circus – by chance, in the train taking them from New York to Chicago. Having arrived a short time before, Baptiste was not yet altogether used to the gasping steel monster, something he'd never seen before he set foot on the mainland and still boarded with a kind of wonder, along with a hint of mistrust. The first time he embarked on it he'd had the impression he was penetrating the entrails of a gigantic metal snake.

Trains often travelled at night and it only added to the strangeness of the journey to speed through a darkness so complete it seemed nearly solid, pierced here and there by the flickering lights of a far-off village, the yellow lamps of small country stations illuminating the deserted platforms. Baptiste sometimes felt that the train was standing still while the landscape was unfolding on the other side of the broad picture windows, like a roll of film – another marvel he'd discovered on North American soil – image by image, in the window frame.

That night, driven by a call of nature, he ventured outside the compartment he shared with Qiu and Quan and explored the rattling narrow corridor. On one side, windows looked onto fields where now and then a farm stood out, or a herd of placid cows, or an occasional thicket of trees; on the other side were doors, all alike, but he thought he remembered that the second-last was the wc. Opening it, he found instead Rochester sitting on a crimson velvet seat next to a slender man whose white shirtsleeves were rolled up to the elbows. His head was bald on top, a deficiency compensated for by a short beard; he had a straight nose, and determined features.

Photos and prints were spread on a table in front of them. Baptiste could see a five-legged calf and an odd creature with a hairy muzzle, scales all over its body, and big flippers.

The two men looked up, surprised, when they spotted Baptiste, who stammered:

"Ex-excuse me, I got lost . . ."

Rochester broke in, fitting onto his face the smile he'd worn the first time they had met, which for the most part, he only took off at bedtime, the way others place their false teeth in a glass on their bedside table.

"James, let me introduce Baptiste Cyparis, whom I'm sure you remember."

"Of course," repeated Bailey absentmindedly, extending to Baptiste a stubby-fingered hand. His gaze was both piercing and dreamy. "Delighted to make your acquaintance, Basil."

Rochester gave a little cough, but Baptiste murmured: "That's all right," and they left it there.

Bailey had nimbly covered the prints with an open newspaper that he now stared at as if he wanted to be sure they wouldn't disappear by magic.

"Can I be of any help to you, dear friend?" Rochester asked Baptiste, who was standing stupidly in the doorway, not knowing how to take his leave.

Intimidated, he said the first thing that came into his mind, which turned out to be the truth.

"Can you tell me where the wc is?"

Bailey raised an eyebrow but Rochester, still grinning broadly, provided the information requested as kindly as a tourist guide questioned about the age of the Sphinx or the height of the Eiffel Tower. Terribly embarrassed, Baptiste thanked him, closed the door and never again set eyes on James Bailey, of whose collection he was one of the rarest gems.

When he went back to his compartment, Qiu was asleep, head nodding in time to the bumps, while Quan, eyes wide open, was gazing out at the night falling beyond the windows, drowning the fields in a bluish twilight that was gradually spreading to the cars. At the sight of them, at once identical and different, the same but given over to contrary states, Baptiste recalled the carnival masks, some of which, from a single physiognomy, expressed fury while on others could be read mirth or sorrow. And then, as the train was speeding towards the gold of the setting sun and plunging into the night. He did not take long to doze off to the muffled sound of wheels on rails and lulled by the swaying motion that reminded him of the sea.

THE BIG TOP WHERE THE MAIN SHOW WAS TAKING place was itself an attraction because it was the most enormous tent ever made. This marvel was illuminated by more than a thousand electric bulbs – three employees had just one task, to check them every day, one at a time, to replace any that were burned out, and to make sure there were always enough spare bulbs. These were carefully wrapped in straw, like eggs, then lined up in wooden crates that almost filled an entire train car. On flat ground, the tent was visible for kilometres around, like a glittering ocean liner on the plain or some monstrous star fallen to earth.

The performances were introduced by lavish scenes from antiquity and biblical times: the Exodus from Egypt, the Massacre of the Innocents, the Wedding Feast at Cana – these religious tableaux needed dozens, even hundreds of extras, essentially interchangeable and for the most part staying a few weeks or months with the circus before leaving to try their luck elsewhere. They travelled together, piled into the most uncomfortable cars, slept crammed into tents they pitched themselves, preparing their own meals outside on small fires that glowed in the night.

Next came the presentation of the Phenomena – the publicity talked sometimes about Monsters, other times about Marvels – that Barnum & Bailey collected the way others accumulate butterflies or rare coins. The Phenomena received a different treatment from that of the extras, nearly as good as that enjoyed by the performers and the tamers. The two groups, however, were carefully kept apart and Baptiste, the bearded lady, and the other oddities of nature were always relegated to the periphery of the camp, not far from the animals.

Clowns, strongmen, acrobats, magicians, wild animals and tamers, elephants and horses were the first real act, sharing the ring in a dangerous ballet; hardly a week went by without complaints of squashed feet, broken hands, or dislocated knees, not to mention the fact that one night, a lion they'd forgotten to feed took a mouthful from the thigh of a horse. Both animals had to be put down before the eyes of the horrified crowd.

Whenever they arrived in a new town or village, while the workers, the stagehands and some of the extras were unloading the wagons and pitching tents and the big top, the procession swung into action, going down the main street to the sound of the brass band under the dazzled eyes of children and those – suspicious but bright with curiosity – of the housewives and passersby who soon flooded into the streets. The procession obviously gave only a general idea of the wonders of the Greatest Show on Earth that the spectators would discover later on, in return for a slight admission fee.

As he was one of the star attractions, Baptiste did not take part in this promotional parade; there was simply an announcement that visitors would have a once-in-a-lifetime opportunity to see with their own eyes "The Most Amazing Man in the World, Sole Survivor of the Worst Calamity to Strike the Planet, A Man Whose Name is Written in Letters of Fire" and, to kindle the crowd's curiosity even more, pictures of erupting volcanoes and devastated cities were held aloft. Baptiste would use that time to say hello to Numa, who always greeted him with half-closed eyes and a husky growl, and to the white manatee, to whom he fed lettuce or spinach swiped from the kitchen, which the animal chewed with a melancholy air.

He rarely joined the other Phenomena, some of whom had regarded him with suspicion from the very first day, as if afraid Baptiste would try to steal their places or oust them from the top of the bill. It's true that the tent where they performed had some of the longest lines, and that shortly after his arrival, the incredible "Vegetable Man," that incomparable artist (who had the remarkable ability to carve, at lightning speed, carrots, potatoes, and humble parsnips into exquisite flowers, ships with sails unfurled, birds whose finest feathers could be seen), had been dismissed. But it was also being whispered that the Vegetable Man had threatened Rochester with the knife that never left his hand and that, with disastrous foolhardiness, he'd even dared to carve a turnip into an unflattering caricature of Mr. Bailey himself, who did not take such matters lightly.

In the middle of this ill-assorted crowd that made up the circus, one part of which was always the same while the other part changed practically from city to city, Baptiste was just as alone as he'd been on his island on the day after the eighth of May. Aside from the few words exchanged every month with Rochester when the latter handed over his pay, in cash, careful to separate the bills before letting them go, his only real conversations were with Elie, Numa the lion, and the manatee. Perhaps because it was so implacably alone of its species, Baptiste had never realized the creature didn't have a name.

One afternoon, Elie took him to meet his mother. Alice was frail, blonde, and grew red as a poppy almost as soon as she caught sight of Baptiste, whom her son had invited for tea. He heard her scold the boy after she'd pulled him hastily into the tent: "I meant a friend your own age, you dolt!" But she reappeared shortly, carrying a teapot and three cups, one of which wasn't chipped at all.

"Sir, I'm delighted," she said softly to Baptiste who held her hand in his cautiously, afraid of crushing her fingers. Above her upper lip was a thin white scar as fine as a thread, which seemed to pull her mouth up very slightly when she smiled, as she did often and ingenuously.

"I would like you to know, this is the first time my son has brought one of his friends home." She broke off, looked around , and moved her hand a little, as if to excuse herself, repeating: "Well, home, in a manner of speaking. . . ." Baptiste realized then that the tent was not uniformly grey but had been patched with countless pieces, some of a solid hue, others with faded patterns; all had, from exposure to the elements, become various tones of beige and grey and dirty white reminiscent of the colour of rain clouds.

The three drank their tea sitting on the grass while the sun went down slowly and moved behind the horizon, plunging the camp into a bluish dimness. They were still there when the first stars appeared. At a gesture from Alice, Baptiste picked up the sleeping Elie and placed him on a pallet spread with a woolen blanket inside the tent. The moon was high in the sky now, round and chalky like a clown's mask. Alice shivered and Baptiste put his arm around the woman's shoulders to warm her.

Quite naturally they became a family, something none of them had ever known, as Alice was an orphan, a child of the circus, while Elie didn't have a father, though spiteful women – one of whom, Jemma, was particularly energetic – claimed that the boy displayed an amazing resemblance to Hector, the wild-animal trainer.

Alice and Elie left their tent for Baptiste's trailer which, strangely, seemed bigger to him once the mother and son had moved in. Soon they settled into a routine, punctuated by the circus's continual moves, the incessant chaos of the tents being pitched and struck, the almost daily performances, the successive crowds of onlookers and the landscapes they never had a chance to explore and that simply formed a changing backdrop.

· · · · · · · ·

They married without delay. Elie served as Baptiste's best man, standing very erect, nearly paralyzed by the solemnity of the event, and Ilsa as Alice's maid of honour. The ceremony, presided over by Rochester, was held outside the big top at dawn, before the procession.

· "But Rochester isn't a priest," Alice had fretted.

Baptiste had shrugged: "I'm not crazy about priests anyway."

She was pretty in the white dress Ilsa had lent her, which the two had spent the night altering to fit Alice's narrow shoulders and slender bosom. Elie had braided a crown of daisies for his mother. She had slipped it onto her forehead; now and then it dropped tiny red ants that she squashed between thumb and forefinger. Baptiste donned the black suit he put on every night when it was time to play the Survivor of the Apocalypse, and he couldn't help feeling a little as if he were doing a performance.

Before them was gathered a small group of no more than fifteen, Jemma having mounted a genuine cabal against this union of a man black as ebony and a woman white as milk, which she described as "an aberration of nature" without noticing that all those to whom she was presenting her argument could have been described in the same way.

The ceremony was brief. There was a document to sign that no one bothered to look at too closely, then champagne to open; but it was not yet noon, the drink was slightly warm and most of the flutes remained half-full after the guests drank the toasts, as they left to get ready for the parade.

Baptiste, Alice, and Elie were now by themselves, all dressed up, in front of the big top where technicians and stagehands were going in and out while the sun beat down. Baptiste was sweating in his black suit; the daisies on Alice's brow were starting to wither, giving off a mild acid smell. She took off the wreath, its imprint staying behind on her like an invisible headband, and it immediately came apart in her fingers. She dove to the ground to try making a bouquet with the scattered flowers, but could retrieve only three slightly bent stems that had at their tips just a yellow heart, as round as an eye. The white petals strewn on the ground suggested tiny boats adrift on the blackness of their shadows, which had shrunk and now were little more than small puddles of darkness at their feet.

FOR ELIE'S ELEVENTH BIRTHDAY, ALICE HAD planned to make a spice cake as she did every year, but Elie had begged that instead they order from the kitchen of the Palace, where they stayed when the circus was in San Francisco, a cake made by the chef himself, its name on the menu the night before looking deliciously mysterious: *devil's food cake*.

The room they'd been assigned was not particularly grand but it was roomier than the trailer they still occupied when they stopped in small towns. A bed with an eiderdown embroidered in burgundy and mustard brown had pride of place in the middle of the room, which contained as well a dressing table with an oval mirror. Baptiste, unaccustomed to looking at his own reflection, always took a moment to recognize himself in it. There was a small sofa and a folding bed for Elie to sleep on, all the furniture sitting on a thick carpet that muffled the slightest sound. Some gilt-framed prints showing Roman ruins bathed in sunlight hung on walls covered with striped wallpaper.

A rare luxury, the three had supper in the hotel restaurant, an immense dining room that had a dozen huge chandeliers hanging from the ceiling, where liveried waiters snaked their way through the tables carrying plates covered with silver domes. Most tables were occupied by circus people. The few other diners looked with stupefaction first at Jemma, who walked with the help of two canes, then at Ilsa, the bottom part of her face modestly covered with a scarf but the abundant growth on her chin still visible; and at Qui and Quan, who each surveyed the room from his own side. As for Baptiste, he was still stunned to see how much attention was being paid to him in the midst of so many more spectacular Phenomena. The people of the fine city of San Francisco were not however in the habit of welcoming dark-skinned people in hotel dining rooms, and the whispers that had greeted Jemma's arrival were transformed into noisy comments when he took his seat with Elie and Alice and laid his black hand on the young woman's white arm.

"I didn't think it was this kind of establishment," remarked a long-faced woman to his left, who started to get up but stopped when Hector entered the room with a martial tread, running his conqueror's eyes over the guests.

The soup was tepid, the roast beef overcooked, and in general the dishes lacked salt, but Elie, unaccustomed to such a feast, devoured everything put in front of him, while Alice was careful to pick up her fork delicately in her right hand once she'd cut her meat with her knife and to dab her lips with her starched serviette after each mouthful. Baptiste could see the husband of the angular woman – who was now twisting her neck to get a look at Bailey at the other end of the hall – out of the corner of his eye. He thought the man looked like Louis XVIII but couldn't remember where he might have seen the face of the French monarch.

Back in their room, the cake was waiting for them, sitting prominently on the dressing table, a dozen slender candles stuck into the white icing. Delighted, Elie turned towards Alice and in a voice that held both reproach and relief, exclaimed:

"I thought you'd forgotten!"

Her only reply was to tousle his hair. He grabbed the knife beside the plates but she stopped him from cutting into the cake right away.

"It's you who forgot something," she reminded him softly as she took a small box wrapped in white paper from her purse. "First, you have to blow out the candles."

He seized the box and opened it cautiously: inside, on a cushion of sky-blue satin, lay a heavy, finely worked silver lighter with, in the middle of some complicated arabesques, a stylized E and C intertwined.

"They're your initials now," she explained, while Elie turned the object over in his fingers, fiddling with the cover which opened and closed with a snap, making the roller, its circumference marked with minute grooves, spin until a spark shot up and then a bluish flame. He lit the candles one by one. She urged him:

"Make a wish."

He looked around at the warm, rich, golden room, his mother and Baptiste smiling, and he knew that all he wanted was for things to go on as they were at this moment. He closed his eyes, breathed, opened his eyes: the twelve flames were out, the blackened wicks of the candles now gave off only some weak smoke. The *twelve* flames.

"There was one too many!" he exclaimed, alarmed, reaching for the offending candle. "Does that mean my wish won't come true?"

Alice and Baptiste had a good laugh.

"No," his mother reassured him. "On the contrary, it means that your wish will be good for two years."

But Elie, unconvinced, looked hard at both of them, sensing a lie.

"I've got something for you too," said Baptiste, thrusting his arm under the bed and taking out a long, wide box wrapped in newspaper, which the boy tore eagerly, revealing a cardboard carton with a coloured illustration of a long train travelling on shining rails through an emerald-green landscape. Overjoyed, Elie spent the next minutes gazing at the various components of the train, properly stowed in their compartments from which he dared not take them. As well as the gleaming locomotive there were eight iron cars, five of them closed, with windows, steps, and wheels in every respect like those on real trains, along with enough lengths of straight rails and curved ones to form, once fitted together, a good-sized ring in the middle of the bedroom rug.

The locomotive started slowly, then speeded up, advancing with a powerful clickety-clack, nearly leaving the track on a curve, just barely landing on its wheels to work up speed again, only to go off the rails for good at the next turn, followed by its cars whose wheels went on turning, pointlessly, long after.

"It doesn't matter," said Baptiste, "we'll try again in a while."

Elie cut the cake after he'd uprooted the eleven remaining candles, tears of wax congealed along the narrow stems, discovering under the white icing a bright red pastry he refused to eat. For long minutes he kept using his lighter to light again the shortest candle and snuff it by pinching the wick between thumb and forefinger. Floating in the air was the odour of ozone, metallic and acid, like the smell after lightning has struck.

IN CERTAIN DUSTY VILLAGES IN THE MIDDLE of the United States, the populace had never seen a black man except in a print or a photo – and those were mostly of convicts, who had expressions so sinister that honest people thus informed about the unfortunate characteristics of the race were determined to be wary of any man whose skin was the colour of coffee.

One night when he was standing, arms folded and one foot slightly forward (a pose he'd borrowed from the lion tamers), in front of a ragged piece of canvas bearing a painting of Mount Pelée erupting, throwing into the sky flaming stones and a fountain of black smoke, Baptiste overheard a conversation between a little girl with blonde curls and her mother, who wore a hat with a broad wingspan that in all likelihood had cost the life of more than one bird and made it impossible to see her face. It was obvious that the lady was a person of some importance in the small town, perhaps the mayor's wife, for the rest of the audience held themselves back

respectfully and sent in her direction looks at once curious and cowed.

"Mama," asked the child in a high little voice, "why is
that man black?"

Baptiste could see that the people around the lady
with the hat were holding their breath as she replied
calmly:

"Because he was burned, my pet. As you can see, he
was in a fire so he's as black as coal. Now come along,
sweetheart, do you want to see the hippopotamus?"

Another night, there were an elderly man and woman
dressed all in black who could have been man and wife or
brother and sister, so much did they resemble one another,
in their bearing more than their features. The two shared
the same stiff posture and an identical look of disap-
proval, with pinched nostrils and mouth. They called
Baptiste *sotto voce* "Satan's lackey," whispering that if he
had survived on Judgment Day it was because God in
His infinite wisdom had not wanted him in His kingdom
and, continuing more and more loudly, declaring that the
colour of his skin was the reflection of his black soul.

"How dare they," the man went on in a tone of bois-
terous lamentation, "present to us here one of those infi-
dels from a land where they know not God? How dare
they corrupt our innocent youth?"

Looking around him, Baptiste observed that the audience was made up of farmers, small merchants, and housewives, all of them well over forty. Brushing aside that detail, he wanted anyway to defend the honour of his island, but when he opened his mouth the man's companion broke into a series of strident *Amens* that drowned out any rectification. In the crowd people began to cross themselves and look worriedly towards the ceiling of the tent, as if they were expecting an answer to come from there.

Profoundly embarrassed, at a loss for what to do, Baptiste tried to attract the attention the workers at the tent entrance, but for the time being they were too engrossed in conversation to realize that he needed help.

The man was still howling what Baptiste took to be passages from the Book of Revelation; a woman flung herself to her knees, two others burst into sobs, a fourth began to ululate. Wanting to calm the hysteria that threatened to settle in for good, Baptiste, unable to think of anything else, began to recite in a loud, clear voice the Lord's Prayer, the first prayer he'd learned as a child, the one that Father Blanchot had made him repeat most often as penance and the only one he remembered in its entirety. As Baptiste was saying it in French, however, the old man, who had never heard the language, began to shout that "the monster is casting an evil spell, calling on the demons from Hell from whence he came in their own

vile language." He was spraying saliva everywhere, its tra-
jectory seeming to imitate that of the projectiles spat
from the mouth of the volcano frozen behind Baptiste in
a spectacular and unchanging fury.

Finally realizing that something was wrong, the ticket
sellers rushed into the tent and tried to escort the man to
the exit, but he struggled so hard that, while the woman
with him was shrieking that people were trying to murder
them, they came to blows. After just a few seconds the
brawl became widespread.

Taking advantage of the chaos, Baptiste pulled with
all his might on a small tear in the canvas between the
volcano and the sea, enlarging it enough to stick his head
and shoulders into it. He raised one foot very high, then
the other, and disappeared through the sky studded with
stars and blazing embers.

Then a strange thing happened to Baptiste. After he had
miraculously escaped the deadly fire that had wiped out
everything and everyone he knew, after people had come
from the United States to invite him to join the Greatest
Show on Earth – for which he was being handsomely
paid – after he had found the family he'd stopped looking
for long ago, then this strange thing happened: he suddenly felt as if his life was finished, over, consumed, and
for the first time he knew what fear felt like.

He began to suffer long bouts of insomnia. He would wake up in the depths of night, shift Alice's arm from where it weighed heavily on his chest, get up, and dress in the shirt and trousers he had been wearing the day of his arrival. He had others now, more than enough to change every day of the week if he felt the urge. Sometimes when he opened the cupboard where they were hanging, he would stand for a moment, disconcerted before such pointless abundance, after which he invariably reached out for the more familiar old rags. Then he would leave as cautiously as he had slipped out of his cell a year before, and walk alone on the deserted site given over now to the dark.

The first time she had seen him don his clothes slowly, mechanically, to leave in the middle of the night, Alice had gotten up and called softly:

"Baptiste, you're a somnambulist."

"What?" He had never heard that word.

"You're walking in your sleep, come back to bed." And standing next to him she had tried to lead him. He'd freed himself with an absentminded movement. It was exactly what he had experienced for weeks now and hadn't been able to name: the impression that he was walking in a dream, or under water, day and night but particularly in the daytime.

"H-how do I stop?"

"Stop what?"

"Sleepwalking. How can I stop?"

"There's just one way. To wake up."

That was useless: wasn't he already awake? A moment later she asked, to be quite sure:

"Are you asleep?"

"I don't know," he replied in all honesty, and went out.

From then on Alice, whom the slightest movement would waken, got up when he'd gone out the door and watched him move away, her forehead against the cold window.

• • • • • • • •

Seeing them all side by side: the mountain of quivering rolls of fat that was Jemma, whose every movement reverberated at length in her white, turquoise-veined flesh, the way a pebble dropped into water gently traces circles that subside as they move away from the centre; the body shared by Qiu and Quan, their two heads, each on its own shoulders, two oranges on a table; the short silhouettes of the midget couple, child-sized but with adult heads, with hair in their ears and hairy genitals in their underwear, who waved their little limbs the way some fish out of water comically twitch their fins; the graceful, perfect figure of Ilsa – until she turned around to show her sow bear's face, which seemed at first to be a joke in bad taste on such a delicate neck; the muscular mass of Ulrich the strongman, whose biceps and triceps bulged under his skin like foreign bodies slipped in between flesh and bone; at the sight of them, hideous and fascinating, Baptiste felt as if he were advancing in a waking nightmare. His life since Mount Pelée seemed to him to be unfolding in a kind of half-sleep where objects, though endowed with their familiar outlines, put up no resistance and allowed themselves to be passed through when he held out a hand to catch them. He took from this insubstantiality the sense that he himself was unreal. Maybe he was still stretched out on the ground in the Saint-Pierre dungeon and all this was just a dream.

MONTHS LATER BAPTISTE, ALONE IN A CELL again, would recall the afternoon when he'd seen her for the first time, suspended between two horses galloping around the track, raising clouds of golden dust that floated a few inches above the black and glossy backs. She had left the first and had not yet grabbed the mane of the second, so when he thought of her he would always have this image: she was flying.

Hair as shiny as the croup of the horses who obeyed the slightest click of her tongue; red lips; wasp-waisted in her sequined costume that reflected the light from the electric bulbs, she was alone with the stallions under the big top. She had headed for Baptiste without hesitating, as if they already knew each other. Above her lips sparkled tiny beads of sweat he longed to lick with the despair of the thirsty man who sticks his tongue out when he feels on his forehead the first drops of rain.

"Are you the Apocalypse?" she asked, examining him

from head to toe with no animosity but no warmth either, rather with a kind of detached curiosity.

Sorry not to be more spectacular, he could only utter painfully:

"Y-y-yes."

"What was it like?"

"I-I don't know. Hot. And then . . . I passed out."

Briskly, she unlaced her fine leather boots and pulled them off like the peel of a fruit, revealing white feet with seashell nails. Continuing on her way barefoot, she let the boots fall in the sand where Baptiste bent over humbly to pick them up, quickening his pace as she was walked away without looking over her shoulder, sure he was following her. He'd had the impression that he was waking from a dream.

With the tips of her white fingers she traced a path down his back where the tangle of scars formed something like a crown of thorns. She had removed his shirt without a word, they had loved one another standing, leaning against one of the posts that held up the tent where the manatee was lapping the lukewarm water in its basin. Then she had gently turned Baptiste over and written on his burnt skin a message that seemed to be engraved in his flesh more deeply than the wound left there by the blazing mountain, like an invocation.

"Does it hurt?"

"No," he lied. But it was only a half-lie, for to feel her fingers on his shoulders, her breath on his neck, he would have suffered a thousand other pains.

Stella lived with Rochester and he shouldn't expect that the events of the afternoon would ever happen again, she explained coldly as she straightened her costume with its shiny sequins. But of course it did happen again: when night had fallen and only the animals were awake, pacing their cages in circles; during the parade when only workers and extras remained on the circus site; in the train car where Stella travelled alone when James Bailey had sent Rochester to recruit some unknown prodigy or new monstrosity.

When he came home, Alice smelled on his breath the brandy he'd drunk with her and her perfume on his fingers, in his hair, on his long legs and in his arms. It seemed to her that if she looked long enough she could distinguish the other woman's reflection in Baptiste's gaze. But she kept her eyes closed and waited until he was asleep to tiptoe out of the trailer and to soap and rinse herself thoroughly.

Baptiste began to attend performances in order to admire Stella at the same time as hundreds, as thousands, of others, feeling a mixture of jealousy and pride at sharing her that way.

The heat inside the big top was infernal; under the ceiling of light bulbs, faces were gleaming, red and stupefied, their open black mouths jagged with stumps of teeth. One could hear gulps and cries of rapture at the arrival in the ring of leather-clad lion tamers, strapped into chains, led by Hector who held a trident like an ancient gladiator or some even older and more formidable Roman demigod. From the ring came smells of sweat, straw, excrement, and chalk dust.

The crowd marvelled noisily at the intelligence of the horse-mathematicians as well as at the intrepidity of the lion tamers. They shivered as they looked up at the tight-rope walkers hanging from their thin trapezes, following with their eyes one who was advancing slowly on a wire, on his chin a stem holding a full cup of tea. But these exploits were too far removed from everyday life to stir in the audience anything but a fleeting and superficial emotion. Laughter was at its peak when the clowns, after a few pirouettes and harmless capers, chose a whipping boy among themselves, going at him fiercely, tripping and sidestepping him over and over until he dropped onto the sand, pretending to help him get up the better to trample him, their monstrously bright red lips on faces painted white opening grotesque grins all the way to their ears.

The spectators recognized themselves finally in both the torturer and the victim and instinctively chose their side. Their laughter rose up, like the snickering of hyenas.

These poor people came to the circus to be filled with wonder; to play at being afraid without having to pit themselves against the danger; to forget for a few hours, a few minutes, an existence that was unbearable or simply dull and hopeless; mainly though they came for the privilege of pointing to and laughing at the bad luck of others more unfortunate than themselves. Of filling their eyes with those freaks of nature observed from a distance, one hand over their mouth as if to stifle a cry. They shuddered, with horror in some cases, but also with curiosity and excitement and with a kind of brief joy they hardly ever experienced, because for one of the rare times in their lives, they were on the right side of things: on the side of those who laughed instead of the laughingstock; on the side of the winners, the virtuous, those who were backed up by the fearsome strength of the majority. Like a powder trail through the crowd, their laughter spread, swelled, and nourished one another. Between this laughter and cries of fright or hatred there was little difference, and anyone who photographed those contorted faces, mouths wide open, eyes screwed up, would have found it hard to tell if they were grimacing in pleasure, in pain, or both. A crowd is never so ugly as when it is laughing.

"Run away with me," said Baptiste, lying on his back with Stella's head on his shoulder, her long honey-coloured hair spread over the black flesh where scars formed pink twists and turns.

Her laugh was crystalline and hard.

"Where to?"

"An-anywhere."

"Why do people always talk about going away and don't care where they arrive or when?"

He felt that she wasn't asking the question of him, so he didn't answer. They were lying on a rough woollen blanket, in a clearing some distance from the camp. The sky was speckled with stars, joined now and then by blinking fireflies. The nearby forest was teeming with mysterious sounds.

"Where are you from?" he asked, because he had just realized that he knew nothing about her.

"From the greyest village in the world, a little dump in Texas, and it's the last place I would want to go back to.

What about you? Do you dream about going back to where you grew up?"

"Where I grew up doesn't exist anymore," he said in a neutral tone.

There could be no reply to that remark. Her finger traced his jaw and his lips. He wanted her again and it was like a raging thirst; he wished he could drink up the night.

"Come away with me," he said, taking her in his arms.

She broke away, raised herself up on an elbow, stared at him and said, seriously this time:

"My life is here, with the horses and Richard – and you. If you want."

It was perfectly normal to come after the horses, for she treasured them more than the pupil of her eye, but coming after Rochester was a bitter blow. A fist tightened in his chest and he wondered if this was what jealousy felt like. Then all at once he understood: he hadn't escaped the Apocalypse; he had succumbed to it like all the others, and this was his punishment.

ELIE HAD SEEN FOR WEEKS NOW THAT HIS mother had been looking haggard, red-eyed, that she startled at the slightest sound and was always checking over her shoulder as if expecting that at any moment a storm would break and beat down on her.

Having seen her happy these past months, he could recognize the opposite of happiness, even though he didn't know the cause. The night before, he'd over-heard a conversation that broke off abruptly when he approached; Alice had been talking about "that siren, that witch, that goddamn creature who's cast a spell over you," in a voice that didn't sound like hers. Baptiste, helpless before her, flipped his hand as if to chase away an insect. He looked guilty but also, strangely, almost happy, as if he were inhabited by a flame that could finally blaze openly.

• • • • • • • •

The heat was overwhelming beneath the heavy cotton sheet of the tent where the manatee was housed. As soon as he entered, sweat began to bead on Baptiste's face, to run onto his neck. Blocks of ice in one corner were supposed to cool the air; he could feel their cold when he moved his arm over them. The ice was melting practically before his eyes, creating a puddle that ran out of the tent in rivulets. He placed his hand, fingers spread, on the translucent surface that was dented and cracked by the heat. At first soothing under his palm, the cold quickly became a bite, then an unbearable burn, but Baptiste forced himself to leave his hand there, and it gradually became numb. When he finally removed it, it seemed no longer to belong to him.

Leaning over the tank of cloudy water, he stuck his fingers into the tepid liquid, which felt scalding to him. He peered at his reflection, at a series of waves that became more marked when the manatee rose to the surface, nostrils closed, velvet eyes wide open as if to greet him. He held out his hand to touch the smooth skin of the creature, which slipped away with a fluid movement of its flippers, then rested his forehead on his folded arms and closed his eyes. After a moment he had the impression that his numb fingers could feel the presence of the manatee, which had silently swum closer again.

In the entrance, a black silhouette against the blinding

light, Elie, who had come to feed the animal, backed up stealthily, heart pounding, careful not to make a sound, and went instead to brush Numa the lion.

He will come back at nightfall, holding tightly in his hand the lighter that will all at once seem infinitely heavy. He will arrange bales of hay in the four corners of the tent, soaked in alcohol he has stolen from the warehouse. Then, with a flick he will lift the lid, turn the small wheel with his thumb, and with a steady hand he will light, one by one, the bales of hay and they will catch fire with a sound like a deep sigh.

Flames rise up in the night, yellow and purple against the black of the sky, the way they appear on the sheet used as a backdrop for Baptiste's act. Sparks blown by the wind soon catch the nearby tents, which are ablaze in an instant. Half-clothed people come running from all sides to get the terrified animals out, and for a moment the scene looks like a phantasmagoria or a carnival. Fire crackles, growls, and spreads in long narrow tongues that unfurl their hundred forked points. The tent where the horses are kept burns from the ground to its frail canvas roof; a stallion, panicking, tears a cloth partition with his teeth and finds the open air. Still blinded by the smoke he runs straight ahead, as if guided by an invisible rider, his blazing mane following him like the tail of a demon comet, along his way knocking over the buckets of water being passed from hand to hand and two stagehands who tried to stop him. His fire-rimmed silhouette finally disappears into the darkness. They will search at dawn for hours, finding neither him nor his remains. The other horses, paralyzed by fear, are motionless as statues, necks strained, nostrils quivering, wild eyes rolling. Numa the lion gets quietly out of his cage, its door left ajar, and walks away, supreme; he won't be seen again either, and Rochester, not really wanting to tell the world that a wild animal has escaped from his menagerie, will be silent about the disappearance when police and firefighters come to question him. Everywhere, animals emerge from their dreamless sleep, adding their shrieks to the whimpers of those that are burning and soon a cacophony of men's cries of rage, women's howling, animals' moaning rises up. Flames climb, dancing like long tresses, just as in the past, deep down in the water, weeds were rocked by the undertow. The fire's reddish glow can be seen from afar, a monstrous imitation of the rising sun, a circle of light glowing like the gilded halos of saints that used to adorn the walls of the cathedral of Saint-Pierre, but now rest jumbled together under the rubble.

Baptiste, distraught, watches as fire devours the world.

No one knows if the manatee died because of the heat or was stifled by the dense smoke, but once the flames were under control, the creature was found floating underwater, inert, its white skin as warm as a human's.

Almost at once, Elie's lighter was discovered in the smoking ash. The boy had dropped it as soon as the last bale of hay was on fire, as if he'd wanted to be sure that it would be easily found. Grasping it delicately with a handkerchief, Jemma brandished it high in the air, asking in a strong voice if anyone recognized it. Alice gulped and Baptiste stepped up like a sleepwalker, saying, "It's mine."

Aside from the dead manatee, the stallion, and Numa the lion who'd mysteriously vanished into thin air, two bears had suffocated and three horses were injured so badly that one had to be shot immediately while the other two looked on, long legs wobbling, hair burned, flesh blackened.

In the crowd of faces – hostile, shocked, or stunned – Baptiste tries in vain to find Stella. Around the horse lying on the sand, limbs still shuddering, a puddle of blood is spreading, drawing under the animal a red and liquid shadow. Nearby, buckets of water are being thrown on the crackling flames still crawling through the grass. In the air drifts a smell that Baptiste recognizes but can't name. Then he spots her, unmoving as a pillar of salt. On her face, worse than hatred, terror, or disgust, he sees sad satisfaction at having been right, suspicion rewarded. While the police are handcuffing him, Alice and Stella make the same move: each places her hands on her belly as if to protect something precious or to hide a source of shame. And then he is taken away and soon it is all as remote, as unreal, as the city buried under the fire of its mountain.

THE DUNGEON IS ICY, AS IF ALL THE HEAT ON earth has been taken away, as if it has never known the light of the sun. Curled up on the cement floor, Baptiste hears cries and insults bursting out of the other cells, joining together to form an incomprehensible din.

A guard advances like an automaton, his heavy black shoes beating time like a lugubrious drum, and stops in front of the metal gate.

Automatically, Baptiste stuffs his hand in his pocket and takes out the copper ball he has carried with him everywhere since his first day with the circus. The sphere slips between his fingers and he watches, doing nothing to hold on to it, as it seems suspended between heaven and earth for a second that never ends.

"Baptiste Cyparis?" asks the guard.

The ball has touched the ground, it rolls down the corridor, disappears.

"No. You're mistaken. My name is Numa, Numa Lazarus," Baptiste says without stuttering.

HARMONY

— OF THE —

SPHERES

As a child, Augustus Edward Hough Love was not so much precocious as different. And to tell the truth, just a bit unsettling. He said his first word at around the same age as his brothers and sisters, but while the older siblings had mumbled the traditional "papa" and "mama," Edward trumpeted a resounding and perfectly clear "fourteen." That was how the story, not totally false but not rigorously true either, that he'd learned to count before he could speak entered the family mythology, a legend his mother kept alive with pride tempered with perplexity.

During the months following that first and founding exclamation, he refused to express himself in any way but by numbers, assigning to each of them one or more meanings known, alas, only to himself.

These seemed to vary according to where the numbers fit in the complicated design the child worked out the way others built towers with their wooden blocks. When finally he agreed to enrich his speech with some nouns and verbs, he continued to show a preference for numbers, pronouncing them slowly, rolling them around in his mouth with delight.

He went through several enigmatic phases when he applied himself to creating series that would allow him to organize the world to his own satisfaction. Going out to the garden to make sure he wasn't doing anything he shouldn't, the nurse would find him sitting quietly in the grass in his short pants, legs stretched out on either side of a pile of loot made up of bird feathers, pebbles, lumps of coal, an old bolt, a piece of shoelace, and what looked very much like a dried-up rabbit's turd, objects with nothing in common except that they were all as black as ink. Another day, he got it in his head to pick up everything round that he could find – including coins his father had left on his chest of drawers and the hoop from his sister's crinoline, scissored out of its envelope of cloth, feats that sentenced him to bed without supper, thus depriving him of the opportunity to add plate, bowl, and saucer to his collection.

Unlike so many little boys, Edward didn't tear open the objects to see how they were made. Rather he would press his ear against anything that interested him, as if he were trying to locate its breathing or its intimate palpitation.

His mother, seeing him motionless like that for the first time, his head against the belly of a rag doll, thought to herself that maybe he had the soul of a physician – after all, that is not an occupation to be sniffed at. When she found him a week later in the same absorbed posture but this time with his temple pressed against a big stone at the back of the garden, she didn't know what to think.

"Edward, what are you doing there?" she asked impatiently.

"Listening," he replied in a low voice, as if to avoid startling a bird.

"Listening to what?"

"To what's underneath."

She went on, determined to get to the bottom of it. "Underneath what?"

He replied, as if it were the most normal thing in the world: "Underneath the rock."

She did not let go, presenting in a tone of cold observation: "Edward, what's underneath the rock is earth."

Now it was the little boy's turn to ask: "And under that?"

"Under what?" Her impatience was growing in spite of herself.

"Under the earth," the child reminded her.

She wondered how the devil her son could have become so obstinate. "Under the earth, young man, there is more earth."

Then, to cut short this discussion that was obviously going nowhere and from which she had no hope of emerging victorious or even of learning more about this small individual to whom she had given birth, she added sharply: "And earth is dirty. Look at yourself. Now hurry and change or you'll be late for tea."

• • • • • • • •

No doubt it was best, all things considered, that little Augustus Edward did not dream of becoming a disciple of Asclepius, for he was so awkward he was often a threat to himself and others. During the first ten years of his life he:

– nearly drowned at the age of nine when he fell head first into the duck pond. It must be said that he was busy just then reading *De motu corporum in girum* by Sir Isaac Newton and that, face buried in the large volume that he was struggling to keep at eye-level, he had been advancing mechanically across the back garden, not watching where he was going. (Incidentally, he nearly drowned a second time when, after a gardener had fished him out *in extremis*, he released a desperate cry and dove back down to look for the book, which, as per the Archimedes Principle – *an object, wholly or partially immersed in a fluid, is buoyed up by a force equal to the weight of the fluid displaced by the object* – had sunk straight to the bottom.)

- had four fingers run over as he was attempting to measure the circumference of a wagon wheel in motion.
- dyed his younger sister's hair an ugly shade of green when trying to give her the blonde tresses she'd been dreaming of, using a concoction he'd prepared from various ingredients only some of which were edible.
- sprained his left ankle at least three times and his right ankle once on the stairs that he climbed up and down absent-mindedly, chanting his sums to the sound of his steps on the marble.
- prepared in the kitchen a mauve mixture that seethed and fumed before producing an abundant foam the dog had the misfortune to taste; the animal spent two days between life and death and afterwards stubbornly refused to place even one paw in the accursed room.
- almost lost an eye while performing before his mother's dressing table mirror a mysterious experiment in optics that involved a pocket handkerchief, two silver spoons, and an oil lamp; he nearly set fire to the family manor into the bargain.

There was a time when he counted everything: the number of times he ran the comb through his crow-black hair every morning; the number of peas on his plate; the number of flagstones in the main foyer (this operation presented an extra challenge, for those that ran along the walls had been cut and he had to reconcile the fractions); the number of footsteps between the house and the duck pond and between pond and chapel. Then he tackled some more difficult matters, endeavouring to estimate with complex formulas how many hairs there were on the dog and pieces of gravel on the paths in the garden, eventually spending weeks with his nose to the sky trying to calculate the quantity of stars in the firmament. Around the same time he began to suffer from migraines.

Even once he'd given up his mania for counting everything to grapple with problems both more wide-ranging and more difficult, at moments of nervous tension, worry, or doubt he kept up the habit of reciting to himself long series of figures that made sense only to him, and that he seemed to invent even as he calculated, chanting:

0, 1, 1, 2, 3, 5, 8, 13, 21, 34, 55, 89, 144, 233 . . .

1 4 1 5 9 2 6 5 3 5 8 9 7 9 3 . . .

. . . or in a case of extreme distress:

6, 28, 496, 8128, 33 550 336, 8 589 869 056, 137 438 691 328 . . .

· · · · · · · ·

The entire Love family got its first strong inkling of its youngest son's remarkable skill at dinner one evening in

April, 1894, when he was twelve years old. On the menu there was mutton, a meat Edward hated because he thought it tasted like wool and he stuffed his portion in his pockets so that later he could give it to the dog.

Theresa Love shared the latest news about the household with her husband, the colonel. He listened abstractedly, having no interest in a visit by a fabric merchant – she had acquired more than ten metres of Italian silk which would be used to make new drapes for the small study – and even less in discussions with the gardener on the location of various roses – a bush supposed to produce red flowers having been covered instead with yellow buds the summer before, so that this spring an entire bed had to be reorganized. She was now at matters of household management, which were still submitted to the head of the household so he could ratify his wife's decisions. He did so methodically, only too happy that she was taking charge of it all, although he nevertheless insisted on having the last word.

"Mary asked for Saturday off to attend the wedding of one of her sisters in Yorkshire," said Mrs. Love. "I told her, 'You poor dear, I don't know how many sisters you have, but if they all decide to marry one after another, each in a more out-of-the-way place than the one before, you'd be well advised to buckle your suitcase for good.' Just think, she's been with us barely eighteen months and already she's been away twice for some such nonsense. I hope she realizes she can't take advantage of our kindness."

"Twenty-two," Edward said in a low voice.

"What's he muttering?" roared the colonel, determined to make a man of this slender and withdrawn son. "Speak up, boy."

"It's not eighteen months that Mary's been with us, it's twenty-two."

"That doesn't matter," continued Theresa who didn't intend to get flustered over such a minor detail.

The colonel, who valued precision in all matters, congratulated Edward, surprising everyone because children were not supposed to join in adults' conversation.

"Well done, son! Twenty-two months. No matter what the circumstances, accuracy is essential."

"Actually," Edward went on, slightly encouraged, "she joined our staff exactly twenty one months, three weeks, and five days ago, but I thought it best to round it out."

Around the table, everyone had stopped chewing. The mutton was congealing on their plates. Wanting to dispel the uneasiness he'd provoked, Edward added affably:

"It was a Monday."

Once the initial surprise was over, the colonel was favourably impressed by such an unusual talent. He sent for calendars of the preceding years, then the twenty-two volumes of the nineteenth edition of the *Encyclopaedia*

Britannica thus far available and questioned his last-born son until the lad's mouth was dry, his head spinning. Not once, however, did the child make a mistake. Without hesitation he could state on what day the Battle of Agincourt had started, on what days Shakespeare and Queen Elizabeth I had died, on what day Christopher Columbus had first set foot on American soil, and even, after a very brief pause, on what day Our Lord was born (Saturday), though that was impossible to confirm.

When they finally got up from the table, the sun had long since disappeared behind the hills. Edward realized then that he had not been able to say the one thing that had struck him as important, the very reason he'd spoken up: both of Mary's absences were not for her sisters' weddings but for their funerals.

• • • • • • • •

The Love boys' private tutor was a thin, melancholy, feverish young man who spent his days writing fiery missives to the woman who had left him for a young man who was not just rich but – supreme outrage – horribly handsome. For the most part then, Edward and his brothers were left to themselves, their teacher content to set before them volumes from the manor's library or his own collection, paper, and pens, and to give them some perfunctory instructions. After that, with his bulging forehead resting on his fine and trembling fingers, he began to search for an adjective to rhyme with *cruel*.

Thus Edward learned Greek and Latin almost on his own, deciphering the original text of the *Iliad* side by side with the Latin version by Lorenzo Valla and the English translation made by William Cowper. Later, he took a certain pleasure in the plays of Seneca until the day his brother Philip informed him that nothing in those works had really occurred.

Accustomed to finding in books a kind of harmony that too often the world seemed to lack, Edward first thought that his brother was joking. Going back to his reading however, he couldn't drive doubt from his mind. What if Achilles and Ulysses had never existed? If Phaedra and Hippolytus were merely chimeras?

"Sir?" he asked faintly.

The slender, pale young man, surprised, lifted his eyes from the page he'd been hunched over all morning.

"What is it, Edward?"

"Sir, *Phaedra* is true though, isn't it?"

A blush coloured the tutor's cheeks. He imagined for an instant the fascinating and fertile discussions he'd dreamed of when accepting the position – Oh, how his life had changed since then! Oh, the cruelty! – on the nature of truth and lies and about the uneasy position between them occupied by literature, even Greek literature. That thought was driven away at once, however, by the image of his beloved in another man's arms, and he gave up on exploring the subject more deeply for the benefit of the young pupil staring at him, round eyes filled with worried expectation, while his older brother, sitting a little farther away, was having a quiet laugh.

"No, Edward, it's not true," he replied bluntly.

"But . . ." the boy started to say.

"It's not true," the teacher hammered out his words. "I'll have you know that just because words are said or even written, it doesn't mean they're true." Then, in a tone of voice he'd have used to reprimand a particularly insolent pupil: "Let that be a lesson to you, young man." Then he began to search for an adjective that rhymed with *treacherous*.

Edward, sheepish, closed Seneca and never opened it again. As of that day he limited himself to books of algebra, arithmetic, and trigonometry, which he was certain could not lie to him.

Edward was awkward and ill-at-ease around other children and adults: the latter regarded him with the brief and superficial attention paid to a phenomenon such as a potato that resembled a human face, or a strongman on display at a fair, the former banned him systematically from their games with the visceral instinct peculiar to all young animals that allows them immediately to distinguish the one in a crowd who is different from the others. He was, however, absolutely at home in the land of mathematics. The quiet purity of numbers, their reassuring predictability, their sensible and sober elegance combined with the infinite possibilities they gradually revealed – like a horizon line that seems very close but moves away when one approaches it – everything that formed the very essence of geometry, algebra, and arithmetic occupied and kept his mind alive, offering him at once a refuge and a journey that was constantly renewed.

Around the age when young boys ordinarily stopped wanting to join in their sisters' games, insisted on having long trousers made to replace their short pants, and started eyeing the youngest and most winsome servants, Edward turned in on himself even more, if such a thing were possible. He went on sharing meals with the family but did so grudgingly and with such stubborn silence that his mother, exasperated, finally excused him, as long as he condescended to sit at the table and appear civil whenever there were guests.

For one autumn and one winter he lived at night, spending solitary hours watching the course of the stars, transcribing it at dawn on large sheets of paper that he then covered with notes and observations. He became

engrossed for weeks at a time in endless equations, enjoying nothing so much as shedding light on their funda-
mental and radiant simplicity, covering entire pages with
his delicate writing, with the *d*, the *q*, and the *b* resembling
notes escaped from a symphony, while the *g*, the *j*, and the
y suggested flowering trees in the spring. Often, he would
fill a piece of paper, turn it over to write on the back
between lines already drawn, then furiously crumple it and
start afresh at once, never wearying or losing heart, convinced that one day what he was looking for would turn
up. He would fumble in the darkness that most often
bathed his mind, but where now and then a brief and searing illumination gave him a glimpse of what he'd worked
on for weeks without knowing it, which had now appeared
to him fully formed, like a bird emerging from its shell.

Stopping one morning to contemplate the exquisite
economy of the Pythagorean Theorem, he challenged
himself to discover every day a new proof to demonstrate
it. He gave up after a few months (following seventy-six
demonstrations) not for want of inspiration but because
he was convinced that he could go on like that for years,
and that more complex problems – though some of them,
such as Fermat's Last Theorem, were similar – required
his attention.

· · · · · · · ·

He was twenty years old when he met the woman who was destined to become his wife at the home of a family friend, where she was spending the summer in order to perfect her English. While the guests were soberly pacing the lawns and talking about politics and horse races (the gentlemen) and the latest styles in hats (the ladies), Edward left the manicured gardens and ventured into the woods next to the property where the atmosphere was cool and dim. He walked aimlessly for a while, thinking distractedly about the best way to estimate the number of branches on a tree and then the number of leaves, when he discovered a clearing where a shape was stretched out on the ground.

Wearing a delicate blouse of ecru silk and a skirt of the same fabric, cinched at the waist with a periwinkle sash, with her parasol at her side, she was lying full length in the grass, her ear pinned to the ground. Edward approached cautiously and inquired politely:

"Excuse me, but are you all right?"

The young girl – for she was one, with eyes as blue as the sky, raspberry lips, teeth like pearls – looked at him sharply, and with a finger on her lips to warn him not to make a sound whispered:

"Very well, thank you. I'm listening."

"And what do you hear?" he asked, his heart beating, murmuring as well.

"I'm fairly certain it's an F sharp," she replied calmly, in the prettiest voice in the world.

They smiled. From that moment, in the too rare sunlight of the English countryside, he knew that he loved and would love Garance (for that was her name) until the day he died.

THOUGH GEORGE AND THERESA LOVE HAD hoped their youngest son would make a more brilliant marriage than the one he was entering – rapturously, so it seemed – with this young Frenchwoman with the lilting accent, who seemed to prefer by far the piano over her domestic responsibilities, they did not oppose it. They were aware that Edward too was an imperfect choice and were, in truth, surprised that he was actually considering marrying at all. They had always feared he would end his days alone, surrounded by collections of minerals, odd optical instruments, even animals mounted on walls. They were therefore more than delighted to see him land a most respectable position at King's College, and to find a small house not far from the University of London and settle there with his young wife, who did not seem at all discouraged by the prospect of such an austere existence.

On the contrary, Garance was enchanted.

They were married on a sunny day in autumn. Seeing her advancing towards him, all blonde and rosy pink in

her gown of forget-me-not blue, Edward felt that the
planets and stars, whose secrets his young wife swore she
could hear, were striking up a celestial nuptial march just
for them. Indeed, that evening they escaped from their
guests through a secret door and found themselves alone
on the grounds of the manor with only trees as their silent
witnesses. Looking up, they discovered that the sky was
shot through with shimmering colours, as if a magician
were taking silk handkerchiefs one by one out of the dark
sleeve of the night. Veils of lilac, mint, fuchsia, and ver-
milion sparkled, luminescent, like marionettes whose
strings had been pulled from very high.

"Those clouds are from Mount Pelée," Edward
announced. "They've travelled across half the planet and
are now over Europe." Then, more pragmatically: "It's
sulphur that gives them those colours."

Garance nodded, but she wasn't fooled: she knew for
certain that it was heaven's gift on their wedding night.

They rented a pretty two-storey townhouse in Pimlico,
with high ceilings and pale wood floors, where daylight
came in through broad windows. Garance couldn't wait
to set up her piano, a bulky instrument assembled by
Nicolas Blanchet himself, which had stood up remarkably well during the crossing of the English Channel. As
if he'd wanted a companion for the colossus filling his

parlour, Edward bought his bride a harp that quickly found its place in the middle of the room. Sometimes, during the first months, he would enter the parlour in the small hours when the room was filling with the early light of dawn and catch sight of the massive silhouette from the corner of his eye. The curve of the harp's frame, echoed by the rounded shape of the piano lid, gave him the impression that he was disturbing a secret meeting between a diplodocus and some fabulous dragon.

The other rooms were furnished with odds and ends, old things brought down from the attic of the Love home where they'd been gathering dust for generations and that Garance enjoyed bringing back to life the way one cultivates a garden. She had spread on the floor two kilims unearthed at some second-hand store; they were threadbare but she swore that the faded colours created richer, deeper shades than the Turkish rugs that were the latest thing. In front of the windows she arranged bushy ferns that traced bright shadows on the white walls, and in the bedroom set two potted orchids side by side. At night, their two flowers, bulbous, ample and velvety, spotted with pinks and purple, mingled their heady perfumes.

• • • • • • • •

Edward's first experiences of teaching – which were also, incidentally, his last – were disappointing. On the morning of his inaugural class he arrived an hour early, arranged around him the volumes, scribblers, textbooks, even the globe he'd brought, and took a close look at the vast amphitheatre soon to be filled with his students. The tiers were arranged in a semicircle, climbing steeply from the teaching platform; a row of windows opening on his right provided a glimpse of tree branches, as the classroom was located on the second floor of a three-storey grey stone pavilion. Once he'd completed a quick examination of the premises, Edward went back to a particularly thorny question that had been bothering him for days and had even wakened him several times in the night. Each time he woke thinking the solution was near, practically within reach, but each time, when sleep drifted away, it had escaped him. He began to jot things in one of his notepads, turning the pages as soon as they were full without rereading them. When he ran out of space, he finally picked up a piece of chalk to continue the demonstration on the board, covering with formulas the words *Augustus Edward Love, Natural Philosophy*, which he'd written there for his students. Those students were starting to arrive in small groups, taking their places, opening their exercise books and waiting for nine o'clock.

Nine o'clock sounded and nothing happened. Engrossed in his demonstration, Edward, who had shed his jacket and rolled up his sleeves, went on filling the boards with marks, some as incomprehensible to his first-year students as the alphabet of a foreign language. Two or three, full of goodwill, did their best to transcribe what they saw before their eyes but gave up after just a few minutes. They opened newspapers, began Latin translations, and at ten o'clock the sixty or so young men silently left the classroom while Edward, who still hadn't turned around, went on writing, wrapped now in a cloud of chalk dust.

The head of the mathematics department came and took him to the teachers' lounge, a room with massive leather armchairs and sofas and subdued lighting. It was dominated by a huge stone fireplace that had on its chimney, engraved in block letters, the words: PROVE EVERYTHING, a motto that seemed aimed at him specifically. He wavered for a moment under that burden, seated across from the department head who asked for black tea, then set out to explain in a kind, fatherly tone tinged with impatience, that Edward must undertake to address himself *to his pupils* and to *explain mathematical and philosophical notions to them* in such a way that they would *understand* them and could *pass their examinations*. He pronounced certain words slowly, articulating them as if Edward were hard of hearing or simple-minded.

Mortified, the young teacher assented. The second class was slightly less disastrous. Only twenty-three of the young men who'd appeared the week before returned that Tuesday morning, most of them looking sullen. With nearly two dozen pairs of eyes focused on him, Edward started the roll call and limp hands went up as he read out the names on his list. He marked an X next to the absent, noticing without realizing it that 62.666 percent of his students were missing.

Those seated in front of him, wearing the regulation grey jacket and trousers, white shirt, and bowtie, seemed resigned.

"Welcome to this class in natural philosophy, where we shall study in particular the relations between nature and mathematics," said Edward without taking a breath. From the tiers of seats, no reaction. Next came a lengthy explanation in which he did his best to present in simple terms the necessary relationship joining mathematics to the natural world from which it stemmed and that it could at the same time depict, model, and explain. A young man in the front row yawned. Those sitting by the windows were looking outside, where squirrels chased each other in the branches of the oak trees. The rest were staring blankly at him.

"Very well," he concluded. "First and foremost, an exercise that will allow me to assess your knowledge and your skills." Quickly, he wrote an equation, a sublime variation on the Pythagorean Theorem. As a child and an adolescent, he had spent hours admiring its simple harmony and exploring its seemingly endless ramifications.

$$a^n + b^n = c^n$$

"Some of you may be familiar with Fermat's Last Theorem . . ." he ventured. If that was so no one breathed a word. A tall, thin student in the back row was staring at the door with a kind of desperation, as if cursing the moment he'd come through it. "It couldn't be simpler," Edward went on, speaking to his chalk. "This equation is true if n equals 1 or 2. For any other whole number other than zero, it is false. If you would, gentlemen, figure a way to prove it."

It was of course impossible, at least in so short a time; generations of mathematicians and scholars of all kinds had done their best to find a way to demonstrate the theorem for which Fermat had jotted hastily in his copy of *Arithmetica* that there existed a simple proof which he could not set out in detail because the narrow margins of the book were too small to contain it. Edward himself had tried for nights at a time but had come up with nothing satisfactory. What was surprising, now that he thought about it, was that no one had ever thought of

challenging Fermat's claim. Maybe he tended to embroi-
der the truth. Or he'd wanted to play a trick on someone,
or else had been quite simply wrong. Be that as it may,
Edward was curious to see what the twenty-three students in front of him would do with it during the hour
granted them.

At the end of the class, all placed the fruit of their
labour on his desk, some handing him thick bundles,
others a single sheet. The results varied: an unsettling
number of students maintained, in a manner more or less
woolly but some apparently sincere, that they'd been able
to resolve the enigma (one punctuated his demonstration
with a triumphant QED); others admitted defeat after
mere minutes and had been content to spend the rest of
the hour doodling (among them was one who had handed
in a rather accomplished drawing of a squirrel eating a
hazelnut); three had submitted a perfectly blank sheet;
and surprisingly, two had been able to prove how the
equation was false when n equalled 2.

At the third class there were only fourteen students facing
Edward. He returned to each of them the exercise from
the week before, with annotations and comments. (The
student who'd executed the drawing of a squirrel received
a mere passing grade for his demonstration but, moved
by a need for justice, Edward had given him a "very good"

for his sketch.) When he started to explain why none of them – regardless of what they thought – had been able to demonstrate Fermat's Last Theorem, he suddenly had a brand-new hunch. It was as if he had always considered the problem in the form of a two-dimensional image that had all at once acquired a third one, leaving the page, as it were, and floating in the air. He could now observe the formula from angles whose existence until then he could not even imagine. Leaving his explanations unfinished, he undertook immediately to note on the board whatever came to mind. Stoically, the students took out journals, Latin translations, and drawings of fauna they had observed, and busied themselves with them till the end of the class.

The department head came back a few hours later, in a foul mood. "I thought we'd already discussed this," he said to Edward, who was gazing, motionless, at the board now entirely covered with formulas, calculations, and notes. "Your task is to prepare the students to *pass their exams*. Not to make them *waste their time* on *insoluble* theorems and then ignore them. I do not care to arrive at this point with my teachers, but things cannot go on like this . . . Unless we are aware of a *profound change* in your teaching methods, we will regretfully . . ." Noticing that Edward wasn't listening he broke off and looked up at the

board where were written the first steps of a demonstration at once simple and subtle and perfectly elegant. For
a moment it took his breath away.

Getting his wits back, the department head inhaled
deeply and suggested amiably, as if it were what he'd been
intending to propose from the outset: "Why not forget
about classes for a few months, dear colleague, and devote
yourself instead to research, since that seems to suit you
better." Only at that moment did Edward seem to become
aware of his presence.

"Excuse me?" he said, blinking.

· · · · · · · ·

Edward didn't give a hoot that Garance had not yet found
a servant to fix their meals and clean the parlour, where
everything aside from the two instruments was covered
with a thin coating of dust. Never would he have considered reproaching her for not seeing to it that curtains
were hung at the windows, or not doing the food shopping, nor did he make a fuss over eating cold ham twice a
day every day of the week.

The house on Alderney Street was a cheerful sham-
bles where notebooks and scraps of paper darkened with
formulas and fragments of musical scores littered armchairs, tables, and counters, along with small stones in

various shapes and colours. Edward collected these and presented them to his wife as others would have offered some silly emerald necklace or a dull diamond ring: tourmaline, which when heated became all by itself a magnet; a tiger's eye with shimmering stripes; two sorts of feldspar, which she liked even more when he told her their names were respectively moonstone and sunstone. Each possessed its own crystalline voice. Of them all, however, her favourite was obsidian. This was a piece of vitrified lava, of a black as dense as the darkness of a hundred nights superimposed in fine layers, mirror smooth, sharp, at once the opposite and the sister of ice. Alone among the stones it was silent, as if the fire that had given birth to the mineral had at the same time snuffed out the breath that lived within.

These stones were to be found on chests of drawers, on carpets, even in their shoes or between their sheets where Garance gathered them. She liked to make them shine brightly in the sunlight and to turn them over and over in her palm until they were exactly the same temperature as her fingers. At the same time, Edward was trying to decipher the musical scores with their scattering of small black marks, just as he used to study the equations of Euler and Gauss. He suspected they described a phenomenon that he had a hunch led if not to the answer, then at least to the question that had been bothering him ever since childhood, even though twenty years later, he still did not know how to name it. Like its occupants, the small house was suspended between heaven and earth, between music and mineral.

GARANCE DETECTED THE SECRET SONG IN ALL things, the intimate, hidden voice; equally alive and inanimate, multiple and singular, infinitely large and ultra small, all in the same way. While she adored music it was not for rest or entertainment or even as a pleasure for the senses, but rather because it offered a respite, substituting a series of predictable, organized sounds for the perpetual flurry she lived in from morning to night, and that followed her into her dreams: the silky swishing of a bird's wing by which you recognized it as much as by its song; the silent call of the snail; the minuscule rustle of a blade of grass bowing in the wind; the pattering of raindrops, each unique, like snowflakes; the tiny sound print of water on earth; the minute crackling of a shoe on the gravel underfoot, that's due not so much to the pebble rubbing on the sole as to inner tensions that pass through rock and hold it together. All forces similar to those that drove the stars above their heads, the singular song of each reverberating in the night, each echoed by those of all the others, similar too to the muted underground rumbling of the planets.

One day Edward asked her to describe that harmony of the spheres. She replied with a question: "Have you ever heard a whale sing?"

"No."

"Me neither," she admitted. "But I've heard it described. It's a strange cry like a combination of many voices, and in it you hear all together water, salt, bones, and flesh, a cry that's at once a lament, a love song, and an invitation to play."

"But the whales are alive," Edward objected. "Heavenly bodies are inanimate."

"But they still turn, don't they? They attract and repel one another, they're born and one day they will die."

"I meant, they haven't all been given the gift of life."

"I know what you meant. But maybe our definition of life is too narrow."

She thought about that for a moment, then went to the cupboard to fetch eight crystal goblets the elder Mrs. Love had brought them, horrified by the absence of proper stemware in the home of her son and daughter-in-law. She filled each one to a different height and made them chime by striking them gently with her fingernail.

"Imagine that instead of eight goblets there are millions," she said. "And that they all chiming at once and that the song of each creates new harmonies in all the others."

"Is that what you hear in heaven?"

"It's what I hear in the earth."

• • • • • • • •

With mischievous pleasure, Garance gave her husband some writings of Pliny the Elder. Edward didn't know what to do with them. Though obviously dictated by a genuine passion for knowledge, they were riddled with errors, misinterpretations, and fabrication; they seemed to him to belong in equal parts to science, which he revered, and literature, which he had learned early on to mistrust. Unable to condemn them as lies once and for all, he obviously couldn't give them credit either, though he did discover in some passages a kind of truth that had little to do with the rigour and precision he generally prized above all else.

Generally people are unaware that by closely watching the sky, master scientists have determined that the three superior stars project fires that when they fall to Earth, are called thunderbolts. Those fires come in particular from the intermediary planet, perhaps because, receiving an excess of humidity from the upper circle and an excess of heat from the lower, it gets rid of it in that way; which is why we say that Jupiter sends down thunderbolts.

Many have tried to calculate the distance of the stars from Earth. They have stated that the Sun himself is nineteen times farther from the Moon than is Moon from Earth. Pythagoras, a shrewd genius, concluded that from Earth to Moon there were 126,000 stages; from Moon to Sun, double that. His opinion was shared by the Roman Gallus Sulpicius.

But sometimes, according to musical relationships, Pythagoras calls the distance between Moon and Earth a tone; from Earth to Mercury, a half-tone; to Venus, more or less the same; from Venus to Sun, a tone and a half; from Sun to Mars, a tone, that is as far as Moon from Earth; from Mars to Jupiter, a half-tone, from Jupiter to Saturn, a half-tone; and from there to the zodiac, a tone and a half.

That makes seven tones, called in its entirety diapason, *or universal harmony.*

Laughing, Garance tried to explain why he might take an interest in these inventions.

"It's like music," she suggested.

"Absolutely not," Edward retorted, cut to the quick. "On the contrary, music is methodical, it doesn't tolerate errors. Of all the arts, including architecture very likely, it is the most mathematical."

"Of course, it respects rules, it originates in calculations and harmonics . . . But do you really think it's the mathematics in music that makes us love Mozart and Bach?"

"I don't know Mozart well enough to say so," he confessed. "But Bach, yes, certainly. You must realize better than anyone that he made frequent use of the Fibonacci sequence and of the golden mean. Even better, with his tremendous interest in numerology, he carefully coded his own name into *The Art of the Fugue*, as if to sign his work indelibly but hidden from laymen—"

"I know all that," Garance broke in impatiently, "but what it hides is, precisely, the essential."

"Which is?"

"Imagine for a moment you've translated *The Art of the Fugue* into numbers, and that you're reading that series of numerals – or even easier, imagine that nothing has ever existed save the score, that it has never been played and never will be, that it is sufficient unto itself . . . Is Bach's genius still present?"

"Of course!"

"How do you know that?"

"It's there in a virtual state, as something latent but complete."

"You see, music is what begins to exist once that virtuality is expressed, which disappears immediately afterwards. Mathematics is nothing but its acts of birth and of death."

He enjoyed being wrong at the end of such discussions, no matter how they were concluded. It seemed to him that Bach always emerged as the winner.

· · · · · · · ·

On Sundays and days when Edward did not go to the university, they explored the town together, visiting every corner on foot, walking along the Thames until they found themselves surrounded by ancient hamlets seemingly unchanged for centuries, where people still lived off carp fished from the brown waters of the river. Avoiding the main roads, they passed through working-class neighbourhoods where faded laundry hung out the windows and children stared at them, eyes widened by curiosity or hunger. Going home, they admired the majestic façades of the opera house and the Royal College of Music. Their favourite walk, though, took them to the British Museum, where they spent whole afternoons getting lost together in exhibition spaces that housed Roman, Egyptian, and Asian artifacts, then ending up in one of the libraries: the Grenville, perhaps, with its narrow, dark wood bookcases behind whose glass doors the books themselves appeared to be treasures, not so much exhibited as protected from indiscreet eyes; or the gigantic Reading Room with its gently curved cerulean ceiling.

There, they plunged into unknown books whose mere existence seemed nearly miraculous. Garance gleaned haphazardly, asking for one gilt-edged volume that attracted her like a jewel; leafing through another with crumbling pages that gave off a white powder and a faintly mouldy smell; consulting a third written in an indecipherable language but with prints eloquent enough for her to reconstitute or invent the story. From their words as from their silences, she drew material for complicated symphonies that she noted on music paper. Conversely, Edward's reading since childhood had respected a single principle from which he had never departed, despite its disadvantage: as soon as he'd finished a book, it imposed five or ten new ones, which meant that his ignorance grew infinitely faster than his meagre knowledge. The principle demanded that whenever a volume referred to another – whether to contradict, praise, support, disclaim, cite, or mock it – he would note the title of this second work on the ever-growing list of books he had to read. Over the years this list had taken on the appearance not simply of a tree whose trunk split into more and more abundant boughs that in turn divided into countless branches, but of an entire forest, where paths wound between luxuriant inflorescences, marking relationships that united the different works and the relative importance of each. Unaware of the passing of time, he would not look up until, surprised, he heard the guard announce that the building was closing, and discovered that the light seeping through the high windows in the blue vault had changed and night had fallen. They would go home then, slightly dazed, each with the impression of returning from a journey to a different continent, which they described as they walked in the setting sun.

One afternoon as they were coming back from a walk in the Victoria Tower Gardens, Garance stopped in front of a tiny display window piled high with rolls of rice paper, a fat, beaming Buddha, two gilded dragons, some jade statuettes, and a large white ornamental vase decorated with blue flowers. Inside, a tiny, wrinkled Chinese woman greeted them with a resounding *ni hao*. Startled, they bowed slightly, hands joined at chest level as they had seen figures do on Japanese prints. The old lady invited them to explore the boutique. Coughing slightly in the cloud of incense, Garance immediately began to rummage among the odds and ends, exclaiming blissfully when she found some exquisite figurines carved from ivory as white as snow and marvelling at a particular bronze vase. Its sides supported eight dragons, heads down, seven of which held in their partially open jaws a metal ball the size of a quail's egg. Beneath them, frogs with gaping mouths were poised to take in the sphere hanging above them. There was nothing especially decorative about the object; also, it was very heavy, as Edward realized when he tried to lift it after his young wife expressed a desire to see it in the light.

Trying to be diplomatic, he pointed to the slightly chipped porcelain vase and exclaimed cheerfully:

"This one is lovely! I'll buy it for you if you want, it would look wonderful on the mantelpiece."

But to no avail. Garance wanted the impractical and cumbersome urn, which Edward had to carry home, stopping at every corner to put it down for a moment, long enough for some energetic stretching exercises under the amused looks of passersby and the delighted gaze of his wife, who was admiring him as if he had slain a genuine dragon of flesh and blood and scales for her. It was well worth the lumbago he knew he would suffer the next day.

Garance's interest in the object didn't stop there. Once it was placed conspicuously in the parlour, she used every means possible to discover where it had come from and what it could be used for. Edward agreed to ask a few colleagues in the Asian Studies department but none could provide the slightest information about the dragon urn, one actually saying that since he had never heard of it, the urn was quite possibly not genuine. That was all it took to drive Edward to consult in chronological order everything the British Museum libraries had on the Jin, Yuan, and Ming dynasties.

When he came back empty-handed from his last bout of research, he finally thought about calling on the old Chinese woman who'd sold it to them, but he came up against a closed door and drawn shutters. According to the shopkeeper next door where Edward had gone for information, the merchant had disappeared, taking with her figurines, porcelain, and oriental vases. She had been replaced by an Italian dealing in prints and antiquarian books.

After this series of setbacks Garance, not satisfied but apparently resigned to never knowing more, nearly succeeded in convincing him that the endless questions surrounding the object only added to its value. As long as they knew nothing of where it came from, how it was used, or how it worked, she explained, it offered infinite possibilities. If they learned just what it was about, it would be sadly reduced to being nothing more than what it was. "Imagine," she concluded, "that someone comes to demonstrate to you by $a + b$ that it's a common tea-kettle or a kind of kitchen scales or, I don't know, simply a child's toy: can you swear that it wouldn't instantly be worth less in your eyes?" Implacable as Garance's logic was (it was true that he would admire the object less – the dragons so exquisitely carved; the delicacy of the mechanism holding the copper spheres above the mouths of the frogs; the movement that seemed almost to bring the creatures to life – if he had found out that he was gazing at a mere spinning top, a simple flowerpot), something in his nature drove him in spite of it all to want to clear up the matter. He refused to agree that ignorance could be preferable to knowledge. "It's not ignorance, it's mystery," protested Garance, smiling. To that he could give no response but a kiss.

IN THE AUTUMN OF THE YEAR 1904, EDWARD
and Garance accompanied Mrs. Love to Bath, where she
had gone for several years now, where the waters, she
assured them, were beneficial to her sciatica. She was usually accompanied by her elder daughter (who suffered
from psoriasis and also swore by the miraculous springs in
the famous spa), who unfortunately was confined to home
because of exhaustion near the end of her pregnancy. And
so Edward and Garance packed their bags, fearing the
worst. The journey lived up to their expectations.

Every morning they followed Theresa Love to the
baths where she soaked for an hour, watch in hand.
Resembling an immense underground cavern, the room
threw back the least murmur with an echo effect that
gave the slightest sound, every word, even a whisper, a
multiplied and magnified presence. The light from the
narrow windows seemed rather to emanate from the
healing waters and was then mirrored on the ceiling.
Every day they found there, strangely devoid of bodies,

the same heads bathing in the watery light and floating on the surface.

The diet the hotel imposed on its guests was Spartan. In addition to the sulphur-smelling water, legendarily rich in minerals, drawn from the Pump Room and served still tepid in long glasses wrapped in dainty white napkins, those taking the waters were presented with a boiled egg in the morning; boiled vegetables at noon; and poached fish in the evening, again accompanied by vegetables cooked in water. Garance, dreaming of roast mutton and spit-roasted chicken, came to muse whether, through a kind of osmosis, those vegetables could be the cause of the greenish tinge that she saw on all the swimmers in the pool.

In this city of old women and long diaphanous young girls, they soon noticed that everyone was walking around with a novel by Jane Austen, once the most famous of its inhabitants, as if her works were an essential guide for making one's way through the city, although the streets were clearly identified. One morning when his mother, eyes closed, was immersed up to her neck in the lukewarm water, breathing deeply as if not to waste an atom of the precious vapour given off by the pool, an incredulous Edward observed three ladies who appeared to be unacquainted, but were sitting in neighbouring chairs along the pool, all plunged deep in *Sense and Sensibility*.

Catching his eye, Garance whispered to him, in a voice just loud enough to travel the distance between them, nevertheless with the result that her words were immediately picked up and amplified by the echo: "You know, Jane Austen hated this place."

He didn't know. Nor, apparently, did the three ladies, who stopped reading for a moment and pricked up their ears in spite of themselves.

"She thought the life here was deadly, society unbearable, the gossip insufferable, and the famous water undrinkable. She'd be horrified to see how she is venerated here, in this place she loathed, and without a doubt by the descendants of those she despised."

Edward, who had never since childhood felt like opening a novel, not having enough hours in a day to read books that would enlighten him concerning the world as it really was without also having to worry about those that held pure ravings, now told himself that he wouldn't have minded a conversation with that Miss Austen.

After a few days, Edward and Garance decided to take advantage of Theresa Love's daily nap to explore the sand and ash-coloured city whose two poles of attraction, impossible to miss or to confuse, were the thermal baths and the theatre. The first was devoted to treating the body;

the second, so they said, to resting the mind, although its programming was generally a letdown, careful as it was not to impose on those taking the waters any entertainments that would have forced them to think too hard.

They went first to admire the Royal Crescent, the city's pride. They stood side by side at the end of the vast and verdant lawn, before the huge structure whose proportions were strangely reminiscent of the winter palaces in certain northern cities. The façade curved in a half-moon shape. They looked at one another, perplexed.

"It looks nice," Edward ventured to say.

"Yes," added Garance. "It's very . . . how can I put it . . . orderly."

He agreed.

But it was when they took it into their heads to walk around the impressive structure that for the first time they felt some affection for the grey spa town. The back of the building was an untidy mix of architectural schools, styles, and periods: while the façades of various dwellings merged to present a single, smooth surface, their backs were adorned with overhangs, gables, corbels, and small round windows as surprising as a red slip showing under an austere mourning dress. Even the roof line was broken by slopes of different angles, and a plethora of dormer windows that were followed at times by half a turret. From then on, they tried to look at the entire town as if it had been built entirely in the manner of the famous cres-cent, like a stage set whose public front was painted but whose back conceals far richer discoveries.

Making the best of it, Edward resolved to study Bath's singular characteristic – those famous hot springs, unique in the country – as attentively and seriously as he would have examined a large-scale phenomenon. As he explained to Garance, "He who fails to discover what is interesting about a drop of water or a grain of sand would be wise to blame it on his microscope or better yet, on his eye, rather than on the object itself."

What fascinated him was not so much the healing powers of the water in question – to tell the truth, he had some doubts on that score – as its temperature when it sprang from the earth, which was practically the same as that of the human body. The water had been heated in the crucible from which all life emerges: it came from the planet's throbbing heart.

Abandoning completely any questions about arithmetic and other basically quantitative problems – which could be solved, he was certain, by a sufficiently powerful count-ing machine – he began to focus all his attention on more complex subjects, those having to do with the specific characteristics of the thing observed and its relationship with the observer. He had long since stopped trying to find out how many leaves a tree could bear, but now he thirsted to understand how the leaves were created. He spent entire days investigating and drawing with the aid of a magnifying glass the foliage of certain ferns with jagged outlines that seemed to be repeated *ad infinitum*, smaller and smaller, with no indication of when the mechanism would stop or even if there would be an end. Next, he thought about the specific architecture of the tree, which allowed it to resist storms that could destroy buildings made of brick and stone, and tried to figure out which of its properties were responsible for its resilience, finally concluding that paradoxically, its strength lay in its weakness – that is, in its flexibility or elasticity. He reread in one sitting everything ever published by Robert Hooke who, in *De Potentia Restitutiva*, had presented as an anagram a proof that was a model of clarity: *Ut tensio, sic vis*. He studied for a while the innermost chemistry of plants, distilling in his laboratory chlorophyll, emerald and transparent in its beaker, the circulatory system of plants reminding him of the human body's: the chlorophyll that irrigated the tree from roots to branches was indeed similar in nearly every respect to the haemoglobin carried by the blood that circulated in the vessels. The whole bore some resemblance to the strange hunch of William Stukeley, who in 1750 had put forward in a book entitled *The Philosophy of Earthquakes*, the idea that "God Almighty had laid their pipes and canals in the earth, from a great depth, even to the surface; like as he has planted the veins, arteries, and glands in an animal body."

Edward was fascinated by the discoveries of Newton, Leibniz, and Laplace, and especially admired the latter's observations on celestial mechanisms, the inclines and eccentricities of orbits as well as the elegant solutions to problems through recourse to the harmonies of spheres. He immediately wanted to explore the multiple facets of the world in the same way, with the help of mathematics, which seemed to him the very instrument that had forged the universe. Like Laplace who, when Napoleon noted that nowhere in his system was there a reference to the Creator of the world, had replied simply: "I had no need of that hypothesis," Edward found it unnecessary to have a supreme architect to explain the universe; architecture was all he needed.

If two centuries earlier a good dose of genius had served to deduce from the fall of an apple the law of gravity and, even more, to evoke the forces that govern the entire solar system, most of the observations made by his contemporaries seemed to Edward unimaginatively descriptive and devoid of any originality. Strolling through the countryside around Bath, notebook in hand, he wondered how to express and thus elucidate the entity that was a tree, or the thorny problem represented by the corolla of a rose. There, it seemed to him, lay the true, the only issue: to invent formulas that could describe in one way or another what it was to be alive on this planet.

A FEW MONTHS AFTER THEY WERE BACK IN London, Edward obtained a modest scholarship to cover their moving expenses and the rent for a room in a most attractive house. That accomplished, they set out for Italy, for the caldaria, tepidaria, and frigidaria of Bath had given him an urge to know those of Pompeii, which now could be seen. It struck him that because of their proximity to the famous volcano and because they dated from a period so remote that it was nearly lost in the mists of time, they must conceal a mystery. Perhaps they would help him elucidate some of the hunches that still came to him with searing intensity, but then vanished before he'd even had time to grab a pencil and note them. What he had always appreciated about mathematics was the limpidity, clarity, and absolute precision conferred by its abstract and theoretical character, freed from reality and its contingencies. Now he was finding everywhere in the physical world applications for the formulas and equations with which he had covered reams of paper during his childhood, which now seemed equivalent to the scales and arpeggios a musician must master before tackling a symphony. Back to his first loves, whose memory had been wakened in him by Garance and her harmony of the spheres, Edward discovered he was fascinated by earth and the invisible forces at play beneath its surface.

Having arrived mid-morning in Naples under a blazing sun, they reached their townhouse where they were expected, and stayed inside until late afternoon, when they walked for a while on the deserted beach. Edward, though he had lived his whole life on an island, felt as if he were regarding the sea for the first time, for the cold, grey expanse surrounding England had very little in common with the green mass, silver-fringed and nearly alive, that stretched out before them. On one side, the shore of the Bay of Naples was plunged in the gold of late afternoon; on the other, the Mediterranean unfurled its long rollers. The air smelled of iodine and ripe fruit. They strode the warm shingle for a long time, then Garance made her way towards the open sea along a nearly invisible spit of land, as if she were walking on the water. Edward followed some distance behind. Both stopped to gaze at the still horizon while the sea before them rose and fell as if following the breath of a gigantic creature.

Turning around after a moment, Edward discovered that the road they had taken was about to be engulfed by the water that covered it, then briefly withdrew before making it disappear once again.

"Time to go back," he said. "The tide's coming in."

But Garance stood there unmoving before the waves that now seemed to surround her on all sides. Holding her shoes, lifting her long cream-coloured skirt, its hem soaked, she remarked seriously:

"Are we sure that the water is rising? Or is the whole earth climbing up to get closer to the sky?"

Amused, Edward wanted to explain terrestrial tides, the combined influences of the Moon and Sun, the force of gravity; but all at once it seemed to him, an islander who'd never actually seen the sea, that neither had he really seen the sky. He took out his notebook and quickly sketched a planet straining vainly towards a star in the middle of a blank page, while Garance let go of her skirt which wrapped around her legs like a ribbon of seaweed, and splashed her way back to him.

After a first dreamless night, they went onto their balcony, which looked out on one slope of Vesuvius. Bread was placed on the table with eggs, their yolks nearly red, strong tea, and a basket of local oranges and grapefruit, called here "fruits of paradise."

Garance sighed deeply with satisfaction as she observed the view of the countryside and the massive outline of the mountain on the horizon. Then, catching sight of a little cloud drifting so close to the summit it could have been a curl of smoke, she inquired:

"Edward, Vesuvius has hardly changed since the eruption at Pompeii if I'm not mistaken?"

"No, my dear, you're not mistaken. Obviously it's hard to judge but documents of the time suggest that it's identical to what it was like two thousand years ago. These oranges are delicious."

"Then what's to stop it from erupting again, Edward, and covering the area with lava and ashes a second time?"

He sipped some tea.

"Well . . . to tell the truth . . . nothing. There've already been around twenty eruptions since the one that buried Pompeii, and even though the last one was nearly twenty-five years ago, as far as we know the volcano is still active."

She mused on that as she grabbed a grapefruit and started to slice it.

"If it can put your mind at rest," Edward went on, "there are usually warning signs before an eruption: seismic tremors, clouds of gas, less significant lava flows and so on, which give the population plenty of time to take shelter . . ."

"I wasn't worried," she replied, then she let out a cry, dropped her knife, jumped to her feet and ran inside, gulping. Edward, bending over automatically to pick up the utensil, spied on his wife's plate, in the pink flesh of the fruit, a mass of blackened pulp with a worm wriggling inside it.

That same morning they headed for Vesuvius, taking the funicular along with two scientists (one, an ophthalmologist by trade and vulcanologist by inclination, bore the curious name Tempest Anderson) and a dozen other tourists, among them two imperturbable Germans and a young French girl who turned green the moment the cabin began to move. Garance did all she could to calm the woman whose husband, himself hardly less anxious, chose to squeeze his eyes shut and take refuge in prayer, his disjointed *Hail Mary*s punctuating their ascent. The contraption, clanking on its cables and iron rails, finally got to the top without mishap. They found there a man with ebony skin who was pacing, alone, the cracked circumference of the crater, eyes down as if he were looking for something in the grey and black earth. His footsteps drew behind him a complicated labyrinth one might have thought he was trying to get out of. Edward greeted him politely but the stranger seemed not to see him.

The travellers spent hours gazing at what was beneath the surface of the soil, looking up now and then to discover, surprised, the city of Naples, spread out at their feet like a tiny construction set, unfolding all the way to the sea. Observing the hard, black, fissured soil, Edward thought for a moment that he could see a crack opening in the deepest part of the crater, revealing a thick magma, orange and seething, which reminded him strangely – was it the persistent smell of sulphur floating above this landscape of fire? – of the turbid water drawn in the Pump Room in Bath.

Edward trudged through the heavy, lead-coloured dust, trying to imagine the depths from where lava had gushed two thousand years earlier. Although they had annihilated the Roman city, the flames had nonetheless carried in their destruction a form of eternal life, because they had been blazing, unchanged, from the dawn of time, like the fire that burned in the Sun and the stars that gazed at them from high in the sky.

After some rather long formalities, the repeated presentation of their passports, the production of letters of reference hand-written by outstanding professors from the universities of London and Oxford, the signing of countless documents written only in Italian but which clearly stated that they undertook not to disturb anything and

not try to take home any statues or mosaics or even pebbles, they were finally able to set out to discover Pompeii,
buried and now half-emerged from the earth, escorted by
a guide only too happy to stretch out in the relative coolness of the shade of a low wall and let them stroll quietly.
Thus they were able to spend several days, from morning
till evening, surveying the streets of the ghost town in
perfect solitude the dig having been interrupted a few
days earlier and due to resume at an indeterminate date.

The recently unearthed thermal baths, which resembled those in Bath, though thousands of kilometres and
two oceans separated them, brought nothing new to
Edward's understanding – unless it was confirmation of
Rome's genius, capable of exporting art and technology
to the most out-of-the-way corners of the Empire.
Nevertheless, here, in the shadow of the volcano, he felt
he was getting close, almost touching the revelation that
kept getting away from him and of which he knew that it
had to do with the secrets of earth and fire.

Incredulous, they peered at the façade of an ancient
bakery where they could read, in clear characters, the list
of breads available from the house; they marvelled at
graffiti a mischievous hand could have drawn the day
before, then quickened their pace, blushing in spite of
themselves at the menus adorned by mosaics illustrating
the various choices offered by the ladies of the night who

shared a house in which each had her own room. Their footsteps rang out in unison along the bumpy cobblestones just as had, two millennia earlier, the heels of men and women of whom nothing now remained but those inscriptions in the stone. As they strolled through this phantom city, both felt as though a certain dread was silenced, leaving room for a kind of serenity. Reliving their visit in memory years afterwards, Edward would see in those walks the happiest hours of his married life.

Garance however had for some ten days been experiencing bouts of weakness that forced her to sit down to catch her breath or sometimes even lie down for a few minutes, the pink in her cheeks turning crimson at the slightest effort, and since the incident with the grapefruit she had complained of losing her appetite. She would retch as she pushed away meats roasted or cooked in sauce, and would eat only foods that were white: white bread, stiffly beaten egg whites, goat cheese, peeled apples, sweetened creamy rice.

Late one afternoon when the sun was casting long, narrow shadows on the ground after beating down all day, she came to a halt, faltering, at a street corner in the deserted city, outside a sand-coloured house. Edward rushed to catch her, but she stepped over a chain loosely hooked onto two wooden posts and entered a square villa whose walls were adorned with portraits of young women carrying baskets overflowing with fruit. Then, without hesitating, walking as confidently as if she were in her own home, she crossed the first rooms, then reached a small bare chamber in the back, with one window that let in the last rays of the sun, bathing everything in a rosy light. There was a low stone berth where she lay down, then folded her hands over her chest. Edward joined her, shivering when the back of his neck touched the cold stone. They lay there for a moment without talking while the sun disappeared slowly into the darkness.

"Listen. Did you hear it?" asked Garance softly.

It was a game they played. Amid the crowd milling at a busy intersection in the heart of London; in the library reading room; on the pond where they sometimes went boating, she forced him to stop and prick up his ear. The first times, taken aback, he could only answer her question in all honesty: "Hundreds of wheels on the paving stones and a neighing horse," or "A number of birds." Garance had patiently peeled away, one by one, the strata of sound covering the unique and nearly imperceptible one (a merchant offering her flowers amid the din of cars and horses, buzzing bees imprisoned behind a display window, an unlucky angler cursing between his teeth, and even – or so she swore – the quiet laugh of the fish that got away) which she wanted to give him as if she had just made it appear, like a magician pulling a rabbit from his hat.

There were few sounds in Pompeii. A lone nightingale produced a few trills, then was quiet, as if confused by its own lyrical flights; a lizard ran to take refuge under a stone; cicadas filled the air with their metallic chirring that blended into the background; a breath of wind passed over the city, light as the inhalation of a sleeping child. Lying on the bed of stone, Edward heard none of them, however; the sounds had disappeared as soon as they entered the square house. He closed his eyes, listened as best he could. He could distinguish nothing now but the subdued throbbing of his blood against his eardrums.

"What do you hear?" asked Garance.

"Nothing," he admitted.

She smiled.

"Exactly."

She fell asleep almost at once and he watched over her until the close of day.

When they got up again, the city had come to life. At the eastern end, where the streets that came out of the earth suddenly stopped, continuing only under layers of rock, gypsies had set up camp and their music rose in the night. Clapping their hands, men and women sitting around a big crackling fire intoned chants that Edward and Garance could understand only partially, where the subject was sun and exile. Among the gypsies, Edward noticed the mysterious man with ebony skin. He wasn't singing. In the middle of the group, eyes half-closed, he was smiling gently as he watched the dancing flames. Over sleeping Pompeii fine white ashes fell.

The next day, when they were at their breakfast table looking out on the now-familiar silhouette of Vesuvius, for the first time seeing its slopes covered with snow, Edward touched on their departure. He had thought that Garance might want to extend their stay but she gave him her agreement almost absentmindedly.

He was pouring tea, reflecting out loud that he would go down to the port after breakfast to see if there might be a ship bound for Marseille over the next few days, when Garance abruptly pushed back her chair and dashed to the bedroom, one hand over her mouth. Worried, Edward followed and saw her rush into the lavatory. He heard sounds of water. Back on the balcony, he examined the table. Perhaps Garance could no longer tolerate the mere sight of coloured food?

When she reappeared, dabbing at her eyes, he helped her sit down and offered her a cup of cold milk. Droplets of sweat stood out on her forehead and her hands trembled very slightly when she brought the white liquid to her lips.

"Garance, are you unwell?" he asked anxiously. "Is something wrong?" Then, suddenly alarmed at the thought she could be suffering from some serious illness she'd hidden from him, he pleaded: "You must tell me, I beg you . . ."

Her sky-blue eyes looked deeply into his, then she announced in a voice that was also trembling a little:

"I'm not sick, Edward, I'm pregnant."

He stopped breathing for a moment that seemed to him to last a century, in the course of which he saw the horizon start dancing until it was nearly diagonal, then lie down again after performing several leaps. Then he stood up, knocking over the jar of jam, which left a red stain on the white tablecloth, and took Garance in his arms. She was crying, but it was with happiness.

Over the next few days, on banknotes and in the margins of books on which he could never concentrate, on bills, tickets, the slightest scrap of paper that turned up and, if none appeared, with his fingertip in the dust covering a piece of furniture or the condensation on a window pane, he wrote the same impossible and miraculous equation:

$$1 + 1 = 3.$$

• • • • • • • •

They went back to London without delay. Edward wouldn't allow Garance to tire herself by carrying anything, even her parasol, which he held over her curly head the way slaves in the past would fan their queen with big palm fronds. Back on Alderney Street, she resumed her music but now whenever he went into the drawing room, Edward could hear her softly explaining its subtleties to an invisible presence.

Meanwhile, he ordered from the Sorbonne dusty tomes by abbé Pierre Bertholon de Saint-Lazare who, along with his research into the electricity of plants, meteors, and the human body, had worked out an unusual theory about the forces that sustain earth's core, going so far as to suggest that if one planted metal rods at a certain depth, they would work like lightning rods and prevent the earthquakes that disturb the subterranean world from spreading by forcing them to concentrate on one precise point. But the abbé was on the wrong track, Edward was sure of it.

He plunged back into the quarrel that two centuries earlier had pitted the Saturnists against the Plutonists, the first reckoning that volcanic eruptions were due to the explosion of coal buried in the earth, which caught fire when pyrite came in contact with water, while the second were of the opinion that at the centre of the planet was a mass of matter in fusion which shot up sporadically through crater chimneys, some massive, some insignificant. But in these models, Edward saw mainly the gaps it was up to him to fill in.

Questions occurred to him all at once, ones he would never have imagined springing from mathematics, as they were absolutely foreign to geometry and even to arithmetic. They dealt with the shape and weight of continents; the movement and action of the tides; the properties of matter when subjected to those forces, the most important being no doubt elasticity. This he set out to study methodically, as he always did, by reviewing the work of his forerunners, only to arrive at a distressing conclusion. The totality of the thinking on the problems of elasticity up to the end of the year 1820 could be summed up as follows: an inadequate theory of inflexion, an erroneous theory of torsion, an unproven theory about the vibration of plates.

In a flash, while he was crossing the street, brushing his teeth, or lacing his shoes, everything would fit together. The thorniest problems would be solved as if by magic, with a symmetry and harmony that seemed themselves to be proof of the validity of a theory in which all the elements came together. Those elements formed an infinitely complex whole with thousands of facets – but then the whole would break up like the image in a kaleidoscope, as if he had rotated the ring and scattered the spangles just as he thought he could finally grasp them. The impression disappeared; he tried in vain to recapture some traces scattered just outside his consciousness; but at least he knew that the Solution was within reach.

Garance, walking pigeon-toed now, taking tiny measured steps, was every day becoming fleshier and enjoying it. One evening, standing in profile next to the globe, her belly matching its curve nearly perfectly, she exclaimed in a voice half-jocular, half-horrified: "I look like a boa that's swallowed a balloon!"

· · · · · · · ·

Soon after that she became a watermelon, then a hot-air balloon, and in the end she no longer said anything, herself astonished to feel the foreign life swelling inside her.

She felt the first pains late one afternoon, but she waited an hour after night had fallen before finally allowing Edward to fetch the midwife who had gone that morning to deliver her own sister-in-law at the other end of town, which was why no one answered his repeated thumps on her door.

He had left Garance in the charge of a neighbour more nervous than she was, who kept repeating as Edward explained the situation: "Ah, my God! We need boiling water," wringing her hands and contorting her face.

From the midwife's house he raced out in search of Doctor Whitfield, a prominent physician who lived not far away in a charming townhouse of golden stones. A butler opened the door to a breathless Edward, who could only say: "My wife . . ." The servant came back shortly, accompanied by the doctor still holding his table napkin. He looked the sweating, gasping Edward up and down, his gaze combining suspicion and boredom, as if the visitor were a travelling salesman. In the background could be heard laughter and the clink of cutlery.

"My wife," repeated Edward, unable to go on.

"Yes, young man, your wife . . . ," encouraged Doctor Whitfield, his expression now reassuring and professional.

"She's going to . . . give birth . . ." Edward finally managed to get out as he tried to seize the doctor by the arm and oblige him to get moving.

"And is she sick?" asked the good doctor.

Edward stopped, taken aback.

"No, but she's about to give birth," he repeated, afraid the doctor had misunderstood him.

"That's very good, my lad. I congratulate you on this happy event. Now run and fetch the midwife, don't waste any time. Good luck," he added as he turned around.

"You don't understand!" Edward cried out, words

that made the doctor frown, for he didn't care to be shown such lack of respect – and what's more, under his own roof. The butler shuddered inwardly, unconsciously straightening himself, stiff as the silver-knobbed canes in an urn by the door.

"The midwife isn't in! You have to come with me."

Now the distraught maniac was trying to tell him what to do. With all the haughtiness at his command, Doctor Whitfield, private physician to several eminent members of Parliament, asked:

"Is the lady one of my patients, Mister . . . Mister?"

"Love," said Edward.

"Love," the physician repeated, as if some error in taste had just been confirmed, one he had suspected from the outset. "Very well, is Mrs. Love a patient of mine?"

"No," confessed Edward, who would never have even thought of lying.

"I see. I'm sure the dear lady, who is in perfect health, will have no trouble giving birth. Hurry back to her, I say, and give her my congratulations. Go, now. I wish you a pleasant evening."

Edward had already turned on his heels. He broke into a run. In the sky the moon, slender as a scythe, was covered with clouds, and a cold rain started to fall.

The neighbour had filled the kettle but seemed not to know what to do with it, or with the two full basins

steaming on the stove. Garance was upstairs in their bedroom, her moans seeping through the closed door. Not
daring to knock, Edward started to pace the landing,
where his shoes left traces of mud.

A few seconds or an hour later, he couldn't have said, a
scream ripped through the air and he finally opened the
door to see Garance half sitting in the bed amid blood-
stained sheets, her skin whiter than the pillows she was
leaning against, her hair spread around her head like the
rays of a star. She looked at him, unseeing. In a corner,
the neighbour was wringing her hands again. In a voice
he didn't recognize, Edward ordered her to run to a doctor,
any doctor, and to bring him back by force if she had to.
He searched his pockets and held out the handful of
crumpled bills he found there.

There was a kind of stillness after she left. Edward
knelt by his wife and cautiously touched her skin, soaked
in sweat and cold as marble. He thought he saw her smile,
then came another shriek, mingled with another lament.

He himself welcomed his daughter into the world,
used his penknife to cut the purple cord that joined her to
her mother, dried her as best he could, then stood up,
euphoric, when Garance, after a brief silence, began to
moan again. Panicking, Edward repeated mechanically the
same movements for the son he'd just been given, laying

him down with his sister, two small perfect, wailing beings, on the breast of his wife, who had stopped breathing.

The room, the window, the sky and the stars beyond pitched like a rudderless boat and drifted off. Edward staggered, bumped into the chest of drawers, fell to his knees. As if the law of gravity had briefly ceased to exist, he saw, slowly, dizzily, the copper balls exit the dragons' jaws to crash into the open mouths, black and monstrous, of the starving frogs. They fell two by two until the last one, an orphan who'd lost its partner, this final phantom sphere seeming to remain suspended for all eternity. They had been together for three years, eight months, one week, and two days.

The doctor arrived shortly, irritated without daring to let it show, then the pastor. The neighbour reappeared now and then with a cup of tea. With half his brain, which absurdly continued to function even though it seemed to him that his heart had stopped beating, Edward wondered if she'd found a use for all the water she'd thought it advisable to boil. People dropped in, some he didn't know, others he did know, none of it made the slightest difference. In the empty sky dark night gave way to grey dawn and an ashen light came into the room.

Far, far away a bird called.

—

It was when he stood by the grave where, in a lavish mahogany box lined with silk and velvet, lay the body of the woman he loved, when he had stopped seeking, when he thought he himself was dead, with his silent babies in his arms, that Edward grasped in a pathetic flash something that had always escaped him: understanding what it meant to be alive on this planet was nothing unless you understood how the planet itself was alive.

Once the grave was filled in, when everyone had left and the infants had been taken away, he knelt on the newly dug earth that made a brown slash in the green grass, then lay on his belly, arms outstretched, and pressed his ear to the ground. During an eternity, all he heard was a humming, gradually transformed into a kind of tinkling that grew until it became deafening. All of Earth rang out like a death knell.

The twins – they were named Hyacinthe and Violette – were entrusted to Mrs. Love who, now in her fifties with nothing to do, played with them like dolls. Edward came now and then to see the little ones, who called him *papa* the way they'd have said *uncle* or *Mr. Mayor* had they been told that it was the name of the visitor who was usually content to look at them without a word and on his way out leave some little pebbles as pretty as marbles.

He made a number of attempts, all without success,

to get to know these tiny creatures born to Garance. When the twins turned four, he came for them one August night so they could admire the Perseids, which Garance had always called the *tears of Saint Lawrence* in honour of the unfortunate saint born at summer's end. She had maintained that the stars were the tears he shed at the same time every year. Sullen and shivering in their nightclothes, barefoot in the cool grass covered with dew, Violette and Hyacinthe stubbornly refused to look up at the sky, the little girl grumbling that, "Grandma never lets us go outside without a bathrobe, she says it's dangerous and we could catch our death of cold," until Edward holds up one finger and whispers:

"Look, there."

Hyacinthe spied the fine line of light and asked doubtfully, as if he suspected some magician's trick:

"What is it?"

"A shooting star."

"Is it falling?"

"It's flying."

Violette began to sob noisily, pressed her fists against her eyes. She only stopped crying when he had tucked them both tightly back into beds so small they looked like furniture for a doll's house. He tiptoed out of the room.

• • • • • • • •

He went on with his work but almost absentmindedly, at times with the impression that someone else was performing through him a task supposed to be his but which brought him neither joy nor satisfaction. Day after day he covered stacks of paper with his spidery writing as if someone else through him were dictating the equations and demonstrations he was simply copying down.

During that time he rarely spoke except to himself, repeating in an undertone the reassuring series of his childhood, to which had been added a new sequence of numbers that ended in a finite manner he refused to accept, whose meaning therefore continued and would forever continue to escape him: 3, 8, 1, 2.

On the street people stepped aside because he was frightening and he smelled bad. At one point he had stopped shaving or changing his clothes, which now, stiff with dirt, created a kind of armour that he never took off, not even to go to bed. Most often he fell asleep at his work table and waking a few hours later, sometimes in the middle of the night, realizing that his greasy hair had smudged the latest formula he'd set down in handwriting that dwindled and slanted down like a drying trickle and left on his cheek a partial and inverted mark. He took notes on anything within reach, finally using his hands themselves, spangling them with numbers and signs that crossed each other and became tangled in an ever-changing labyrinth.

Inaugurating a new notebook with a stiff cover that made a grim cracking sound when he opened it for the first time, he finally set out to note the fruits of his labour, his complete theory. He inscribed in blue ink on the first page the following words: *Mathematical Theory of Elasticity*, and kept writing until he had covered the last page and as soon as it was turned, started a new one. Under his pen sprang up the volcanoes and earthquakes he'd been pursuing for years, that he felt he had briefly managed to imprison in his inkwell, before setting them free and fixing them once and for all on the page, the way one pins butterflies to paper. It was all there finally: fire and water; Earth and Moon joined by the tides in which their mingled breaths were combined; waves that made both earth and beings quake; music and silence that united to give birth to the mysterious song of the world that was their most perfect incarnation, Garance herself who in those lines, inspired by her from first to last, would continue to survive beyond both their deaths.

Then one day, without having to reread what he'd produced over the previous weeks, he knew he had finished. The certainty was a relief. He placed the thousands of manuscript pages and the five notebooks on the dressing table, next to the dragons and the frogs that were waiting, jaws agape. Then he lay down fully clothed on his bed amid the silence of the deserted house, as he had lain down years before in the Italian villa taken from the earth. He was found the next morning, eyes wide-open, his hand gripping a grain of obsidian.

LOVE

WAVES

It is barely snowing on Mount Royal. Maple branches – big hands with splayed fingers – reach for the sky. The winter sun filtering between the clouds polishes the trunks of beech trees; hanging from a thin twig, a single bronze-coloured leaf flutters in the wind like a tiny flag. A young birch grows on the edge of the path, its trunk a light brown, nearly pink, that pales and whitens as it grows farther from the earth and plunges into the sky. The mountain top is still bathed in bright light, its base already drowned in shadow.

She exhales clouds of mist in front of her; the breath that escapes from the noses and open mouths of the dogs wraps them in a fine haze. The cold is biting. The path is still nearly unsullied, the snow broken through by just one trail, tracks indistinct but regular, small craters whose powdery edges are collapsing inwards. Without realizing it, she tries to place her feet on them but her rhythm is broken, the distance between steps too great. Lazy and playful, Vladimir, Estragon, and the others wait for her to lead the way, happy to be rooting around in the fluffy snow where they sometimes find a piece of branch and fight over it with mock-threatening barks and growls. Damocles brings up the rear, as if it were his mission to watch over them all, his quick bark calling to stragglers. The long morning shadows are a faded blue against the white surface. Squirrels don't show themselves, huddled in their nests in the highest branches, like sailors' look-outs at the summit of those gnarled poles. Midway into the climb, the silhouettes of alders begin to stand out against the snow like the more and more widely spaced rungs of a ladder that go from dark to light.

Bare, the trees appear more clearly as what they are: mirror and infinite reflection of themselves, the smallest bough, the slightest branch takes on in miniature the tapering shape of the trunk. The branches rise towards the sky with the same movement, the same formation as the roots diving into the ground. As though driven by a similar force, each part is a faithful copy of the whole, present, in a state of possibility, in each of them, the apple tree bearing the apple, the apple, in the secrecy of its heart, the tree.

She wonders briefly what a universe would be like in which humans were made so that every deed, every word contained and revealed them entirely, then reflects that nothing proves this is not the case.

Slightly winded, she goes on climbing, hollowing out
alongside the first trail a second series of tracks whose
outline blurs as soon as she lifts her foot, just as a hole in
the sand is filled in as soon as it's formed. When she
reaches the clearing at the halfway point, where all that
can be seen are a few brown stems, dry and stiff, sticking
out of the snow, she realizes vaguely that if there is only
one set of footprints, it means that someone has gone up
and not come down.

· · · · · · · ·

Freezing rain falls all evening and all night; the next
morning, the trees are covered with a thin, glittering film.
The narrowest stems and trunks that line the path curve
gently to form an arbour under which she sometimes has
to bow her head to advance. The branches she parts as
she goes on, weighed down and made supple by the ice,
tinkle like clinking glasses. A white sun shines in the perfectly blue sky and the forest shimmers under its rays, as
if someone has taken the trouble to decorate every one of
the wild saplings with sparkling ornaments. At the edge
of the path, under a smooth coating of frozen snow, large
chunks of bark resemble driftwood run aground. A few
bushes still bear red autumn fruit, now imprisoned in
transparent shells, as if preserved for all eternity in amber

made of water. At the summit of the mountain, she finds the beech tree, diamond-covered, its branches like garlands of silver and glass.

She stops for a moment to gaze at the landscape spread out before her – flat roofs covered with snow; steaming toy-sized cars; the verdigris steeple of the church of Saint-Germain; the trees sparkling in the sun; a few tiny, rushing pedestrians. But that day, on the big flat rock under the beech tree where she usually sits for a few moments before continuing along the rocky path to the university, stands an inukshuk, firmly planted on two short splayed legs, one long arm parallel to the ground, the small square head sitting on a solid neck. It is a paler grey than the rock it stands on, composed of stones each a different shade from its neighbours. She contemplates it, then whistles to round up the dogs now chasing each other, noses to the ground, paws covered with snow.

Floating in the air the following day is a very fine dusting of snow that glitters in the sun and flashes silver as it dances along tiny invisible currents, like schools of fish moving together in their thousands, all at the same time showing their black eyes or the glint of their bellies. At the edge of the clearing, metal posts of different heights and sizes have been driven into the ground and someone has left a section of fence with lozenge-shaped links.

At the summit, the inukshuk from the day before has disappeared, and now a new man of stone stands at the foot of the tree as if he has grown there overnight. This one is made of the same dozen stones, arranged this time to create a silhouette that one might meet on the street. All the same, she wonders briefly if her eyes are playing tricks on her, if she hadn't observed the little sculpture the day before carelessly or made a mistake recalling its shape. The day after that, her doubts melt away: a third inukshuk, this one more slender and, strangely, nearly ethereal stands in the shadow of the beech branches as if it had stopped there to rest.

From then on, when she climbs the winding path to the summit with the barking dogs she wonders what new little figure will be waiting for them. Every day brings a new one, different yet always made from the same stones, and she has the impression of finding a long-lost friend, whose features she can make out under a series of masks.

In spite of herself she now looks with a certain curiosity at those she meets on her way up or down, trying to imagine them kneeling at the foot of the beech tree, assembling the stones like the pieces of a puzzle. She often sees the same faces: an actress she recognizes from commercials but whose name she can't recall, who walks, always alone, repeating in a low voice, with different intonations, the

lines she is learning; two or three joggers in black track-
suits and huge hiking boots that make their feet look like
astronauts'; a man around forty, his whole body covered
with a kind of plastic or rubber armour, head enclosed to
the chin in something like a medieval helmet, astride a
mountain bike and pulling behind him a tiny bichon
white as snow; an old lady who leans on a long, gnarled
stick as she walks, who greets her with a smile every time
and also greets the dogs one by one; others, too, whom
she only sees now and again, young adults with back-
packs, probably on their way to the university; hikers on
snowshoes with ski poles, and sometimes walkie-talkies,
carrying bags no doubt stuffed with energy bars, bottled
water, even flares; birdwatchers lugging heavy cameras
and lenses that look like telescopes. Does she want to recognize a man or a woman? She doesn't know, and soon
decides not even to try finding out, satisfied to discover in
the shadow of the beech tree every morning a form at
once new and familiar.

Most of the time she is alone on the mountain with the
dogs, a few birds, some ever-present trees and the capricious winter sun, as if in a realm hidden from the city and
that belongs only to her. Against the wash of the sky, the
black branches seem traced in India ink. Veils of snow
hide them for a moment before revealing them again,

naked and petrified by the cold. Seen from the summit,
the entire concrete structure of the Sanctuaire du Mont-
Royal is a beige and bloated scar crushing the houses surrounding it with its mass, a gigantic cement creature
winding through the trees, its curves reminiscent of some
sea monster that haunts sailors' legends.

While Vladimir, Estragon, and Lili are pursuing one
another in the scraggy bushes, stirring up plumes of snow,
and the others are waiting calmly for her to give the signal
for the descent, she finally bends towards the inukshuk,
lifts away its little head – oblong that day – its broad neck,
the flat stone that represents its arms and part of its torso,
its legs, and even its one big foot. Rearranging those same
stones, she erects a miniature statue with a wide skirt, a
slender waist, and a long neck.

The next day she finds a small man made of those
stones in the shadow of the beech tree, but near him
stands a mound of new ones, like an invitation. Mechanically piling them according to their size and the way they
naturally fit together, she thinks about the tall, slim silhouettes by Giacometti she has seen in a book. They gave
off, along with a faintly quivering fragility, a nearly magnetic force, inseparable from their obvious delicacy.

At first she tries to assemble one of those willowy
shapes that seem to be perched on the long legs of a
wading bird, but she must abandon it almost at once: the

stones won't follow such a fractured line, and the flimsy structure collapses before it's completed. She considers making instead a wooden man, using some of the broken branches strewn on the ground, ones that resemble the fleshless limbs she's trying to reproduce. Then, taking one last look at the small mound of stones, she has an idea. She selects four of more or less the same size and arranges them two by two so that they rest against each other the way two playing cards are stood face-to-face to start a house. On these pairs of legs she sets a long flat stone, and atop one end she adds a final one, whose slightly pointed end suggests the muzzle of a dog.

This novelty seems to be taken as an invitation to play because on the following days, she finds at the foot of the beech tree: a heavy turtle with a rounded shell; a ship with three smokestacks, the second one slightly wobbly; a long-necked animal that could be a fat giraffe or a thin dinosaur; and, one morning, a small silhouette of stones with slightly deformed wings that looks like the guardian of everything that came before.

· · · · · · · ·

To the right of the path that she walks every day she finds three new metal posts equidistant from one another.

Someone has begun to unroll an iron fence between them. Vladimir and Estragon, intrigued, stick their muzzles into the links, trying to see through with the stupefied gaze of animals in a zoo. Nearby, in black letters on a freshly planted white sign, can be read:

This wooded area known as Saint-Jean-Baptiste is the property of Mount Royal Cemetery. It is strictly forbidden to build fires, ride mountain bikes, or walk outside the paths. Dogs must be leashed at all times. New works will connect this area with the rest of the network of paths on Mount Royal by 2011.

At the bottom of the sign were a fire and a bike, each in its red circle with a line of the same colour through it; next to them, this time surrounded by a green circle, a dog and its master were joined, most appropriately by a black line supposed to represent the authorized accessory. Briefly, she pictures herself holding the leashes of six dogs capering around her and sees a maypole with peasants and shepherd girls in their Sunday best, skipping merrily around it, each holding the end of a long ribbon that they weave together to create a multicoloured braid.

Damocles stops at the notice too, sniffing it cautiously with a suspicious air. He circles it slowly, lifts his leg, and begins to water the base with a powerful golden stream.

She lets him finish before calling him softly and giving him a biscuit that he downs in one gulp, unflappable.

"It's cold enough to split nails, cold enough to freeze the balls of a brass monkey, cold as a witch's tit, cold like there's no tomorrow, cold as a penguin's toes, cold as the heart of an iceberg," she recites as she climbs the path under the downy flakes that give the dogs white coats.

Vladimir and Estragon wear identical mittens, flame red, and they lift their feet good and high with every step, like circus horses. Doormat the basset hound, feet likewise covered but in blue, has legs so short the snow comes halfway up to his chest and he advances like a submarine, now and then sticking out his black nose to breathe. To scrape up the maximum of powdery snow, Damocles moves his nose just above the ground, mouth wide open like a whale snapping up plankton.

When she has nearly reached the summit, still invisible in the screen of snow, a big bird, its white wings speckled in very pale beige, goes by in a velvet rustling above her head. It's flying low, with a slow steady beating of wings nearly as wide as the path. She looks up to catch a glimpse of its light-coloured breast and tries to keep her eyes on it through the large wet snowflakes that fill the sky, but it soon disappears, a white form that dissolves into the white of the surrounding forest. For a

long time, she searches the highest branches and those
that provide the best view for glimpse of its silhouette.
She finally spots it a little farther away, calm, unmoving,
on a gravestone. She heads for it, stepping cautiously.
The dogs follow her in silence, as if they understand that
the bird is liable to take fright and fly away. When she
finally reaches the stone where she thought she'd seen it,
she realizes that it is the delicately carved statue of a
granite angel with folded wings, face turned towards the
ground and covered with a thin coat of snow as fine as
down, like a veil that moulds its features, revealing more
than concealing them.

White masses break away from the treetops and collapse
on the ground with a sound like a pillow. The spines of
the blackthorns are covered with a padding that masks
their points. Holding out her hand to brush one she
slashes her thumb but only notices it later when she looks
down, surprised to see on the white wool of her mitten a
delicate flower of blood.

At the top of the mountain she leaves behind a little
woman, lame, lacking an arm, standing lop-sided on uneven
legs. When she sees her again the next day, the woman is
leaning against a new inukshuk that serves as a crutch.

• • • • • • • •

A few days later, near the summit, she spies a hooded figure from behind, busy attaching to the cemetery's iron gate a new sign that shows a dog with a red line through it.

"So you're making the forest off-limits to dogs?" she can't stop herself from yelling indignantly. "What will you do next? Track the foxes that dare to put a paw down on your precious ground? Set snares to trap the moles and hares that spoil your lawns? Wouldn't it be easier to just pour concrete over everything?"

She used the formal *vous* with him.

The dogs, who have sensed the irritation in her voice, now add theirs and the end of her question is lost in a cacophony of yelping and growling. Eventually the figure turns around. Of his face only the eyes can be seen, blue slits. She couldn't say why but she would swear that he's much younger than she'd first thought.

"Are you talking to me?" he asks through the scarf that covers his nose and mouth. "How come the *vous*? Do you think there's more than one of me?"

"I mean you and everybody like you."

Then, she can't resist:

"In case you didn't learn this in school, the second person plural is used to show respect when one meets a stranger, or to establish a distance."

"So how come you're saying *tu* now?"

"I'm n . . . That's not the point. This sign talks about

a 'mountain interpretive route,' and those prohibitions, those markers — it's ridiculous. What do you want to build here — a tiny little Disney World for hikers? Will you put a turnstile at the entrance and require hard hats on everyone who's prepared — at his own risk, naturally! — to venture into the woods where you've already driven away anything that might be alive?"

He looks at her, unblinking. Then, never taking his eyes off her, he observes:

"I think your dogs are cold."

She looks down at Damocles and Doormat. Both look pitiful, standing on three legs, the fourth raised in a silent gesture of reproach. She whistles at them and is about to leave when he points out in the same tone:

"You're saying *vous* again. For respect or distance?"

She shrugs and leaves, not looking back. He shouts after her:

"Last month a dog ran away in the middle of the night and wound up here. He fell into a grave that had been dug in the autumn, broke a leg and couldn't get out. He was found two days later, frozen to death."

She has stopped to listen to him; now she whirls around, beside herself:

"Do you think I'm an idiot with your lost dog stories! Do you think every puppy dog that sees your sign will turn around and go home? That's ludicrous!"

"No, but if their owners stop bringing them here to run maybe they won't try to come back by themselves in the middle of the night . . . Don't you think?"

Inexplicably, she doesn't know what to reply. She walks away, dignified, the pack of hounds at her heels.

WHAT DOES SHE DO WHEN SHE ISN'T PACING the mountain? Tries to read. Draws from memory or from life her trees and her dogs in a few quick pencil strokes that are never altogether satisfactory. Forces herself to eat a piece of fruit. Takes short naps, wakes up with her fatigue and anxiety intact. Swears approximately once a month that she's going to put some order into her house and into her life. Starts by arranging her books in alphabetical order. Invariably stops at *B*, exhausted. Spends whole nights watching without seeing them old black-and-white films or infomercials vaunting an exercise machine or a rotisserie – once, under a weird impulse, even ordering the object in question by telephone, throwing it in the garbage still wrapped when it arrived two weeks later. Spends hours looking silently at colour photos, chases away the images that have been tormenting her like a swarm of flies for months, hears the same music again and again, in a loop that suddenly ends, listens in the dark to her own irregular heartbeat, like the

wings of a distraught bird, rests her head against Damocles'
warm flank.

She feels as if she is suffocating, suddenly dizzy inside
the brick walls of her house with its too few windows,
and only starts breathing again once she's outside, under
the enamel sky, on the mountain of ice, surrounded by
dogs, hurrying towards a little man made of stones.

She had never lived with a dog till Damocles. As a child
she'd briefly had two mice that disappeared under mysterious circumstances – one morning the cage was found
open and empty – and a series of goldfish all named
Bubulle that had the unfortunate habit of jumping out of
their bowl, drawing graceful and merciless arcs that landed
them right on the carpet. But no cat or dog that left messes
all over, besides demanding constant care, as her mother
kept saying; for good measure she claimed to be allergic to
hair, fur, and all woollen materials, aside from soft cash-
mere, which curiously didn't set off the terrible attacks of
sneezing that the mere sight of a poodle would provoke.
None had ever entered the house and it wouldn't have
occurred to her that she was missing anything.

She had spotted him for the first time on the street
leading to the SPCA, at the end of a leash held by an exas-
perated-looking young man. With his head thrown back,
firmly planted on his long legs, the dog refused to move

forward. He sat down, moaned, then got up again to take
three steps and resume his game. The man struggled in
vain to cajole him with a biscuit, but the dog stiffened,
tried again to sit down, breathing noisily. Pink muzzle,
velvet eyes: he resembled a young calf.

When she approached him, the animal had raised his
nose slightly and stared at her with brown eyes holding a
nameless sorrow. She'd stopped, gently petted the black-
and white head that came almost up to her hips. He
relaxed, agreed to take a few steps at her side, then pulled
back again when she'd gone by. The man was growing
impatient, pulling harder on the leash, which tautened,
upsetting the dog without persuading him to advance.
He muttered something between his teeth, kicked the
ground a few times, and finally fastened the leash around
a stop sign before moving on without turning around.
Incredulous, she watched him get into his car and drive
away at top speed.

The dog had stopped pulling on the leash and had
lain down, hind legs unfolded on either side of his flanks,
front legs forward like the Sphinx. His chin was on the
ground and he watched the car until it disappeared, then
closed his eyes, gave a long moan. For a moment she'd
thought he was dead. She approached him and sat down
at his side. He slowly lifted his neck and rested his enormous head on her elbow.

"What's your name?" she asked him.

The dog didn't answer but turned his eyes her way, as if he were the one waiting for an answer.

"Marmaduke? Scooby-Doo?"

No reaction.

"Poochie?"

Raised eyebrows.

"Fido? Médor? Zeus?"

One ear half-cocked.

"Elvis? Victor Hugo? Disaster? Dumbo?"

The animal had leaned his head to one side and let out something that could pass for trumpeting.

"Dumbo, really? I suggest Victor Hugo and you pick the elephant?"

She carefully untied the leash and stood up, hoping the dog would do the same. He didn't, staying obstinately supine, head turned towards where the car had disappeared a few minutes earlier, like a compass needle that refuses to change course. Resigned, she sat down beside him again, rested her head on his shoulder and waited.

A mother and her young son emerged from the brick building of the SPCA. The boy was holding a brand new leash attached to a rumpled little white dog that kept leaping into the air. Child and dog were making shrill cries while the mother glanced back as though wondering if it was too late to change her mind. A couple was leaving, carrying a small cardboard box pierced with holes that contained a furiously meowing cat.

People brought dogs, kittens, hamsters, rabbits. There was even a pigeon with a broken wing, carried cautiously by a white-gloved policeman. Some were crying on their way inside and dry-eyed when they reappeared, going away with a lighter tread. Others were stoical when they pushed open the door but emerged shattered. Most appeared simply indifferent. As for the animals, they seemed to know where they were being taken and a few steps from the entrance, the cats bristled, tails up, spitting and trying to get away, while the dogs kept moving but with their heads down, looking defeated.

They spent the morning and part of the afternoon sitting in the grass at the foot of the sign. At one point she'd gone to buy a bottle of water, hurrying in spite of herself for fear of returning to discover that the dog had disappeared. But he was still there, enormous, silent, motionless, and when she offered him the bottle he drained it in two gulps, then thanked her with a lick. Evening was approaching when the dog finally got up and, with what seemed like an enormous effort, turned his head away from where he'd last seen the car he had arrived in. She had started walking and he'd followed with no trouble, politely adjusting his long strides to her steps.

Then, unwisely, she said: "We're going home now."

The dog seemed to leave the earth, pulling her along in a gliding leap and she was only able to regain her balance thanks to years of experience on a trapeze. Then he was galloping, floppy ears beating the air, and even though she pulled on the leash with all her might, she couldn't slow him down.

"Dumbo, I'm giving you a new name: Damocles," she announced, laughing and running at his side.

"And I'll have to find a way to slow you down," she added almost at once.

THIS MORNING THE FOREST IS CREAKING, grating, cracking in the wind like a boat in a storm. The wind floats above the woods, coming from all sides at once as if it were the breathing of the thousand trees that sway, stiff, in the gusts, with a hiss like what one hears when pressing an ear against a shell that still holds a memory of the sea.

The sun is a pale disk, its light struggling to pierce a hole in the white veil of the sky. As soon as the church bell of Saint-Germain has sounded noon, the shadows on the mountain lengthen. Trunks and branches draw a tangle of bluish lines on the ground, the light falls at an angle and already there is a sense of the approach of evening. On a tree trunk struck by lightning a few months earlier, now lying by the path, a pileated woodpecker is jabbing away with its beak. Curious, he turns his automaton's head when he hears the dogs arrive, but doesn't fuss over such a little thing, merely fans his red crest, perhaps as a warning. His long, strangely disarticulated neck

reminds her of Audubon's drawings, those winged creatures shot down then suspended from wires in grotesque
positions as if the painter, unable to bring himself to
choose, had wanted to reveal all in one image the birds'
particularities seen full face, in profile, from the back. The
bird continues to hit the trunk from which he doesn't
seem to pull the tiniest worm. Though without much
hope, she is waiting until the dogs are busy elsewhere –
Doormat has decided to dig a hole into which he disappears almost completely and the others watch, intrigued,
as the snow flies up between his paws – to throw a few
cookie crumbs at the woodpecker. He turns around slowly
and stares at her with contempt, then bends his neck to
snatch them up.

The snow has the texture of coarse salt and it rolls underfoot like thousands of transparent marbles. The thawing
and melting reveal in successive layers leaves, twigs, seeds,
wizened fruit, scraps of bark, bits of grit, cones, maple
keys, acorns, leaves of grass that she discovers in the
reverse order to that in which they were buried, a tiny,
seasonal archaeology whose strata correspond to snow-
storms and freezing rain. The dogs are happy to find bits
of wood that had disappeared months earlier and apparently have lost none of their attraction. Now and then the
loose snow gives way under the weight of Damocles, who

has trouble extricating himself, one long leg after the other, from the icy ground on top of which he remembers walking all winter. At the tips of the maple branches there are slight swellings, not yet buds, reminiscent of scales: oval forms similar to tree-coloured olives.

On the side more exposed to the sun the snow has already melted in the undergrowth and the last hard patches form ephemeral continents separated by seas that can be crossed in one stride. All that remains of the path is a long white strip winding through the trees like a glacier that every day shrinks and recedes some more, leaving in its wake a moraine of small bits of flotsam dragged here by the frost, then abandoned, set down flat on the snow as on the blank pages of a herbarium.

On this day of almost-spring, she discovers on the flat rock in the shadow of the beech tree not a little man made of stones but a boy of flesh and blood, with unruly blonde hair, a heavy checked jacket open over a dirty T-shirt, shapeless jeans, and work boots, deep in a thick book. Right away she feels impatience and a certain disappointment; she realizes that since morning she has been thinking about the statue she will leave on the summit of the mountain at the end of her climb, and she's annoyed with this intruder for keeping her from this very small daily activity that's become necessary for her. She lingers for a while, hoping he'll go away and leave the field open, pretends to straighten a collar, unnecessarily inspects a paw, looks for non-existent burrs in Lili's long coat. On the highest branch of the tallest maple two crows are having a complicated dialogue of clicking and cooing, black gossips warming their plumage in the sun.

He didn't take his eyes off the book at the approach of the dogs and still doesn't seem to notice them prowling about, noses in the air, at a respectful distance. After a few long minutes he finally gets up, closing the volume – an old library copy, its blue cover with gilt letters reading *The Last Days of St. Pierre: The Volcanic Disaster That Claimed Thirty Thousand Lives*. Then, turning around distractedly he leans across to brush the inukshuk he'd been sitting beside and, in a few seconds, puts together a new stone statue. He gazes at it for a moment after he straightens up. Only then does she see the blue of his eyes.

She turns on her heels immediately to go down without even giving the dogs time to catch their breath, as if she'd been caught doing something she shouldn't.

FOR TWO WEEKS NOW SHE HAS BEEN FINDING him at the summit every day, sometimes busying himself with some invisible task among the tombstones but most often at the foot of the budding tree where he settles down to read. She is now so accustomed to discovering him there that on this day she senses his absence before she is aware of it, the way one knows while pushing open a door that the house one is about to enter is empty.

She sits on the stone where she can see the mountain and the landscape below through his eyes. Then a silhouette appears from behind the shed that she recognizes without needing to turn her head. She is watching the foot of the slope, the ballet of the students hurrying towards the music school, miniature characters some of whom are carrying black instrument cases as tall as they are.

He sits down beside her, scratches Damocles behind the ears when the dog trots over to them. Takes from a backpack a thermos of tea, pours a little of the scalding liquid into a tin cup which he holds out to her without a word or a glance, then serves himself. The hot drink has a very light aroma of flowers and smoke. The sun, which for days has only trickled through a veil of white clouds, ventures a ray, then another, gilding the landscape with the brightness of the approaching summer.

Once she has drunk the tea, she sets the cup on the stone and gets ready to leave. "Thanks," she says, and he looks up at her, blinking. She walks away, whistling for the dogs, and he follows them with his eyes for a long time before opening his book and going back to the underground worlds of Pompeii and Herculaneum.

IN THE 18TH CENTURY, AFTER THE CHANCE rediscovery of the buried cities, men worked underground like moles, proceeding laboriously through a network of tunnels and galleries they dug as they went along. Most of the passageways linking one site under excavation (bakery, thermal baths, chamber or atrium of a villa) with another (restaurant, mill) weren't wide enough to let the workers move around, upright or even on all fours, so they crawled like blind earthworms between the rooms and the buildings of what had been, two thousand years earlier, the city of Pompeii. When they reached the outside wall of a new structure, rather than go along it, clearing the way until they found a window, a door, or another opening, they knocked down part of the wall so they could get inside right away. Once they had roughly cleared the room, they would sometimes realize that they had damaged a fresco beyond repair. Still, they uncovered enough mosaics and paintings that they could go on choosing from among them those most worthy of being brought up to the surface. Grottoes were summarily fitted out, where workers came to show the foreman fragments of their discoveries. If a piece was considered to be of inferior quality or execution, it was unceremoniously chopped into pieces. The more ordinary frescoes, or ones that were so numerous that there was no need to bring new ones into the open air suffered the same fate. The various objects extracted from the hard lava and the volcanic dust that had been compressed until it was hard as rock – amphorae, furniture, urns, even food sometimes found intact on the table where the mistress of the house or a slave, dead soon afterwards, had placed them, like the four miraculous eggs whose thin shells had survived the volcano's fire and were nearly fossilized – were similarly subjected to a cursory examination. Jewellery and other articles made of precious metals were set aside to be brought up at day's end and everything related more to curiosity than treasure was rejected at once. In the event that the accumulated deposits in a particular room or building couldn't be cut into with a pick or a mattock, the unworkable zone was abandoned and the men moved on to another. Once the inventory was drawn up and the valuable objects taken away, labourers quickly filled the rooms again with debris so they could move on without having to remove it from underground. Rather tons of earth, gravel, and blackened lava simply moved from one house to another, following the workers' progress so that, aside from corridors along which they could move, no more than three or four houses were ever free of rubble at the same time, as if they had resolved, like Penelope, to undo after nightfall the work accomplished during the day. Thus months after the work had begun, Pompeii was still buried, even doubly: the first time by the volcano, the second by men.

The way into the ruins was via a shaft similar to the one at the mouth of a mine but that, instead of leading to veins of precious metals or deposits of rare minerals, gave access to a vanished time from which one brought back up intact – nearly alive still – remains twenty centuries old, as fishermen bring their nets to the surface in the morning full of shining fish.

The men worked day and night in galleries where air and light were equally rare. The city once buried by fire was now ruled by cold that made the workers' and peasants' teeth chatter, accustomed as they were to the sun of Naples. After several hours their eyes would grow used to the dark that was pierced here and there by lamps, but they went on coughing long after returning to the surface. Blowing their noses on their shirtsleeves, they saw there fine, black soot that might have just emerged from the mouth of the volcano.

—

Nearly every possible object of daily life, from plates to jewels to bakers' implements to those of the ladies of the night, had been exhumed from the ruins of Pompeii and Herculaneum. All that was missing, cruelly, were the men, the women, the children who had lived within those walls, the merchants and priestesses, thieves and fishermen, magistrates, and slaves.

No more than a hundred and fifty years ago, Giuseppe Fiorelli had dreamed up a way to rescue them from the buried city, along with their dogs, cats, and hens, the rats that haunted their granaries and the carp that were served at their tables, all fragile chains of carbon shattered by gases, mummified in lava, and fallen into dust over the centuries.

It was a simple matter of pouring plaster into hollows that corresponded in every respect to the shape of the creature immobilized for all eternity in its setting of petrified magma. This produced silhouettes always different, each one unique, inverted replicas with exactly the outward appearance of a living being, formed around the very absence of that which had given them birth.

On some of these casts can be seen the facial features, the expressions – horrified, serene, indifferent, dumbfounded, resigned – of the inhabitants of Pompeii at the very moment when Vesuvius erupted. Those individuals, eternally paralyzed in the abandonment of sleep

or in the urgency of flight, all seem to offer a silent warning. Some raise their arms towards the sky whence comes
death, while others huddle, trying to protect what they
hold most dear: their child or their gold. Others still are
petrified in a desperate and unmoving race, like the
white-faced mimes and Pierrots who can be seen at street
corners, where they hold the same pose for hours, waiting
for the toss of a coin.

· · · · · · · ·

There are at least a thousand active volcanoes on earth
and probably more under the sea; at any moment twenty
or so are erupting.

The southernmost volcano still active on the planet is
called Mount Erebus. It was baptized (like its brother,
now extinct, Mount Terror) in honour of the two ships
commanded by Sir James Ross who, assisted by Francis
Crozier, discovered them in 1841 during a long voyage of
Antarctic exploration intended to reconnoitre and study
earth's magnetism. For the ancient Greeks, Erebus, the
incarnation of darkness, was the brother of Night. Of
their union were born Aether (Light) and Hemera (Day),
who in turn gave birth to Thalassa, the Sea.

Mounts Terror and Erebus rise like ships run aground
on Ross Island, in the sea of the same name (both testify

to a certain lack of imagination – or perhaps to an incorrigible narcissism on the captain's part). Francis Crozier received no similar honour but some hundred years later, his name was given to a lunar crater near the Sea of Fertility, which may once have housed a volcano.

Still, it seems that most of the cirques and craters that pit the surface of the Moon were not caused by volcanoes but have been hollowed out by asteroids that have crashed on the surface: by a fire that came not from inside, but from outside.

THE AIR HAS A SWEETNESS THAT WASN'T THERE
the day before, suggesting winter is nearing its end. Above
the roofs glides a bluish mist that gives the impression
the sky has leaned over the earth for a moment to see
what was going on there.

The path where the snow melts by day and freezes
every night gleams in the sun like a skating rink. Cautious,
Vladimir and Estragon zigzag through the trees in places
where the hard surface still provides some purchase.
Damocles sprawls full length, paws spread wide like
Bambi's, once, then twice, and pulls himself up, moaning
indignantly. For months he will hold on to his fear of
shiny surfaces and refuse to set foot on a polished marble
floor. Mornings, as on every river, minuscule twigs, bits of
dried leaves, red maple keys are adrift, sailing down the
current to the bottom of the mountain.

Once tea has been served and the first mouthful
drunk, he points with his chin at the dogs chasing each
other in what is left of the melting snow.

"Are they all yours?"

"No. Just one."

"Which?"

"Guess."

The two Labradors, one blond, the other chocolate, the first an exact copy of the second, run in circles, sending up sprays of wet snow behind their stubby legs. Now and then one produces a high-pitched yelp to which the other replies in the same tone. A little behind them, a long basset hound is busy digging a muddy hole into which he disappears almost completely and from which emerge briefly just one clawed foot and one ear.

He hesitates, continues his examination.

A pointer with a silvery coat carefully sniffs the trunk of a tree, walks around it with dainty, measured steps. She twitches when she hears a branch snap nearby as a squirrel steps on it, turns to show two round eyes, their metallic colour exactly the same as that of the short silky hair on her face.

"Juliette," she introduces her. "And this," – points to the hole where a white paintbrush wriggles at the end of a black tail – "is Doormat. Over there, Vladimir and Estragon. These are Lili and Damocles," she says finally, indicating a bichon frise with a black nose, wearing a red coat with her little white feet sticking out of it, who has just yanked a stick from the mouth of an enormous animal who lets out a heartrending sigh, then lies down and covers his eyes with an immense paw as if he wants to say that he's had enough of this cruel life.

"Lili?" he asks, looking at the elongated shape, the long paws drawn up to the body in an unnatural posture one might see on an animal stuffed by a taxidermist who works too fast or is a poor observer.

"That's Damocles," she corrects him.

Hearing his name, the animal looks up and frowns attentively. The bichon, meanwhile, is energetically gnawing her loot.

"What kind is it?"

"A mix of Great Dane, Irish wolfhound, Rhodesian ridgeback, and Neapolitan mastiff," she replies.

Observing it more closely, zone by zone one might say, he does see in the animal the powerful frame of the Great Dane, the huge head and jaws of the mastiff, the strange backbone that gives its name to the ridgeback, and a rough goatee he must have inherited from his Irish ancestors. But there's also some camel in this dog, and some dragon, and probably some hippogryph too.

"What does he weigh?" he inquires, deciding to start with the easiest question.

"I don't know. When he was around eight months old he broke the veterinarian's scale. At the time he weighed seventy-five kilos."

"How old is he now?"

"Three."

"Interesting."

• • • • • • • •

Vladimir and Estragon, the two stocky, cheerful Labradors, belong to a university professor who doesn't care for walking and is only too happy to let someone else spend her days chasing the dogs to make them use up some of the energy they would otherwise expend in mad pursuit of each other, claws clicking on the polished floors of his duplex. Actually, the professor in question isn't all that fond of animals; the labs were bought at the entreaties of an old girlfriend, twenty years younger, who for a while had threatened to want a child, a vague desire he'd skilfully deflected and at the same time fulfilled with a gift of two adorable little balls of fur with curls at their necks, in a basket.

As she was intending to name them Nougat and Nutella, he'd had to intervene and give them names he wouldn't blush to pronounce on those rare occasions when he was the one who must round them up. For as long as the relationship lasted, Marie-Lune – another ridiculous name, but in that case there was nothing he could do – had been happy to take responsibility for the dogs, looking after their slightest needs. She walked them morning, noon, and night, fed them the finest organic kibble enriched with omega-3 – "those dogs eat better than we do," he invariably complained when paying the astronomical pet shop bills, words that she heard, rightly, more as a criticism of her own mediocre culinary skills than of the sums invested in dog food – scrupulously took them to the vet every year for treatments against fleas and heartworm, took them as well every two months to the grooming parlour from which they came home with claws clipped and buffed, scented with an eau de toilette that, she explained to him very seriously, had been blended specially for canines and was called *Oh my dog!*

When she announced she was leaving him – having presumably found a man who didn't grind his teeth when the words *start a family* came up, a hunch that was confirmed a few months later when he ran into her on the street, very pregnant and absolutely radiant   he was surprised that she had stubbornly refused to take the dogs. It would have been too painful, she'd explained at first, to have before her eyes all the time a souvenir, a witness of their relationship; then, as he seemed unconvinced, she had declared once and for all that the dogs needed a house and a garden, that they would be miserably unhappy in a small, second-floor apartment in Plateau Mont-Royal and that she couldn't bring herself to torture them like that. Before this double argument that was based on both her happiness and that of Vladimir and Estragon (thank God he'd been firm; at least he wasn't stuck with Nougat and Nutella), he could only accept. And look for someone to walk the dogs.

Lili belongs to a woman with an unpronounceable name, whom she'd privately christened "Lili Lady" and addressed simply as "Madame." Lili Lady lives on the ground floor of a three-storey brick house, she has silvery white hair like snow in moonlight, small blue eyes that recently have become cloudy. She occasionally has trouble recognizing her dog-walker, calling her sometimes "Anna" and sometimes "Martha." Often the old lady invites her in and offers her cookies from an old tin box that smells musty. She accepts politely, slips the cookies into her pockets, and later gives them to Damocles, who sniffs them cautiously before swallowing them in a mouthful.

Lili Lady's apartment is cluttered with all kinds of objects – small china figurines of shepherdesses or pipers, jardinières in which spider plants with yellow leaves are withering, throws covering the arms and backs of easy chairs, decorative plates hanging on the kitchen wall next to old black-and-white photos of unsmiling people looking straight at the lens. There are several examples of everything: cheap rugs scattered on the beige carpet; three

TV sets lined up in order of size in the imitation oak cabinet in the living room; down to the rolls of paper towels that she glimpses in the kitchen when Lili Lady, who insists on making tea, looks for the kettle. The air smells faintly of roses, dust, and wet wool. Damocles and Lili are stretched out full-length between kitchen and living room, the curly little white dog between the enormous paws of the mastodon.

One day while Lili Lady makes tea, she gets up to look at the books that form an odd collection around the TV sets. Most are in English, a few – knitting instructions and a dictionary – in French, and a dozen others in a language so strange she can't even recognize the characters. She thinks they are novels but she couldn't say why; the covers have no illustrations. She opens one, leafs through it: it is printed from right to left, from top to bottom. Suddenly a cuckoo can be heard, sounding the half-hour.

"Do you take sugar, Anna dear?" asks Lili Lady from the kitchen, over the gurgling of the kettle.

"Yes, please," she replies, immediately returning the book to the shelf.

Then she spots, face-down, a book with a gilt-edged leather cover, its title in solid square letters: PHILOSOPHY OF EARTHQUAKES.

"What did you find there?" asks the old lady, who arrives bearing a tray on which a china teapot with small yellow flowers clinks against matching cups, saucers, and milk jug.

She shows Lili Lady the book, who looks at it closely, turning it over and over in her trembling fingers as if seeing it for the first time. Meanwhile, she pours tea into the old lady's cup and her own, to which she adds a small spoonful of sugar.

Lili Lady holds out the book: "Take it, Anna, you'll make better use of it than I will." She protests but the old lady won't hear a word, so she slips the book into the pocket of her coat, drying on the radiator. Lili Lady seems delighted, inquires about people the girl has never heard of and whom the old lady seems to have lost track of ages ago. She chirps like a bird, moves jerkily to tuck a lock of hair away from her forehead or to pick up her saucer, and repeats several times: "Anna, I haven't seen you in such a long time, I'm so happy." She dares not correct her.

She sips some tea, immediately wants to spit it out but restrains herself and manages to swallow, even smile politely. The sugar bowl has been filled with salt.

· · · · · · · ·

The next day, sitting at the foot of the beech tree, they take turns piling the stones, as if building a house of cards that collapses regularly, lashed by the dogs' tails or when Damocles gallops too close, his steps making the rock quake.

He takes a sandwich from his bag, gulps it down in three bites. Inside the backpack she can make out a new pile of books, some with titles half-visible: *Reflections on Volcanic Mountains, De Vesuviano incendio nuntius.*

"So, you only read books about volcanoes?"

"No."

"What else?"

"Umm – earthquakes . . ."

She ponders for a moment, starts to say something, stops. Sighs, then asks:

"All right, tell me something."

"What?"

"Anything. Tell me what you read this morning."

"No luck. This morning I looked through a gardening book with instructions for transplanting a holly. I can share what I learned with you if you want: first you must choose a spot that's not too sunny, where the soil retains its moisture . . ."

"I'm serious, tell me something that would make me like volcanoes."

"Make you like them?"

The idea seemed to astonish him. He stuffs his hand into his backpack again and takes out an orange, peels it, and softly calls Damocles, who approaches, intrigued. He holds out a section of fruit and the dog shakes his head as if he's just been sprayed, then looks at him with an expression at once disappointed and insulted.

"Okay then," she goes on, "something that would help me understand them. Actually, dogs can't stand citrus. Bring a biscuit next time."

"Mmm."

He seems to be weighing the advice. He shyly offers her a piece of orange, which she accepts while watching him out of the corner of her eye. His skin is golden from spending his days outside, his hands red and covered with calluses and scratches. He bites his nails. Maybe he caught her examining him; he curls his fingers and announces:

"All right. The worst, the most lethal volcanic eruptions – the ones that produce little or no lava flow but whose craters literally explode with clouds of toxic gases – are named for Pliny," he begins, stretching as though he needs to warm up before dealing with the subject.

She is at once happy and surprised to recognize the name. Maybe it won't be just about magma and tectonic plates.

"A Roman, right? A philosopher?"

"Two, even. There's Pliny the Elder, author of a natural history in no fewer than thirty-seven volumes. Then there's his nephew, Pliny the Younger."

"And which one is volcanic?"

"The Elder."

"I assume he was the first to observe one of those eruptions?"

"Possibly. But that's not where the name comes from. During the eruption of Vesuvius in the year 79, Pliny went to see friends who lived in Stabies, some distance from the volcano. If we can believe the account his nephew wrote in a letter to Tacitus about his illustrious uncle's final hours, they dined copiously and went to bed with full bellies. They would never again see the sun rise."

"What happened?"

"What do you think?"

"Vesuvius turned out to be closer than they imagined?"

"That's right. The wind turned and the volcano's fumes asphyxiated the city. Pliny and his friends attempted to escape by sea, but they died on the shore. When his body was found at the end of the 19th century, he was still holding a bundle of documents."

"But how do they know it was his body they found, nearly twenty centuries later? What was in those documents?"

"I've no idea. Still, it was in his honour that the Plinian volcanoes got their names."

"It makes no sense to name a volcano after someone who believed in it so little that he went to die in the middle of a poisoned cloud when he could have stayed peacefully at home. Are you sure there's no other explanation?"

"I'm afraid not."

"And it doesn't bother you that some things are named for people they killed?"

She realizes how her question could be an accusation and adds in a milder tone:

"It doesn't matter."

He has the strange impression that she is forgiving him, and that he's just passed some kind of test.

From her own bag she takes the book Lili Lady gave her.

"Here, I found this for you," she says, handing him the old copy of *The Philosophy of Earthquakes*.

He takes it carefully, gently turns the friable pages that smell faintly of mildew and iodine, looks for the publication date, careful not to damage the binding. While he is leafing through the book, something falls out of it. Curious, she bends down to pick up a rectangle of yellowed paper. Faded colours show horses hitched to curving sleighs dashing through fir trees and a few tall birches in a snowy landscape. She thinks at first that she can recognize from the stiff and formal gait of the horses – which look like circus animals, each with one leg raised very high and bent at a ninety-degree angle, manes neatly combed – the tiny, bundled-up figures in the sleighs and, particularly, the feeling of cold it gives off, a Krieghoff painting. Once she deciphers the title, however, she realizes that it's an old postcard with hand-painted blues, yellows, and browns that give it an aura of unreality rather than add to its verisimilitude. SLEIGH RIDE ON MOUNT ROYAL, FEBRUARY 1910 is printed under the picture. On the back, a woman's hand has written in violet ink:

October 4, 1943. First snow and Arthur left today for the war.
A.

"Tell me," she says after thinking it over for a moment and studying the landscape around them, "is Mount Royal an extinct volcano?"

"No. Why?"

"Why isn't it a volcano? Isn't it up to *you* to tell *me*?"

"I was wondering why you thought it was an extinct volcano. I imagine that even if you walk all over it every day you've never personally witnessed an eruption, right? A small lava flow maybe, a little cloud of smoke?"

"Very funny. I don't know where I got that. It's the kind of thing everyone knows without knowing where it came from."

"So it's the kind of thing to be avoided like the plague."

"And you're personally familiar with the plague? You've experienced it maybe? Rats? Buboes?"

Offended, he replies:

"It's not the same thing at all. We know the plague existed, we know what caused it, how it was transmitted, we know the symptoms, we can calculate the number of deaths it caused."

"Maybe *you* know. As for me, I choose to believe you. The way I choose to believe that Mount Royal was once a volcano and that today we walk around the periphery of an old crater that long ago spat fire and rocks." With her fingers she mimes a spectacular explosion in miniature. "Besides, when you look at the mountain from Dunlop Avenue, or de Vimy, don't you think that it looks like a kind of big sleeping dragon?"

He stares at her, perplexed.

"Do you also think that Mount Royal is an extinct dragon?"

"Not extinct. Sleeping."

THE CITY GREW UP AROUND THE MOUNTAIN
that has stood in the middle of the island since the
beginning of time. Or at least since the Mesozoic Era,
when igneous rocks stole their way into the adjacent
sedimentary layer, then were isolated by erosion at the
end of the Cretaceous Era to create the Monteregian
Hills, the "royal mountains," sole remaining witnesses to
that far-off time. Amerindians grew squash and corn
there and gathered mayapples, prized for their invigo-
rating qualities; they carved into the bark of trees mysterious signs that some old people still declare they saw
as children, on the ancient elms whose shadows bathed
their houses. A thousand years after the birth and execution of Jesus Christ, the Iroquois were already burying
their dead there. It was on one of its summits that, in
1643, Paul de Chomedey, Sieur de Maisonneuve, planted
a wooden cross to give thanks to God for having spared
the newly founded Ville-Marie from the floods that had
wreaked havoc all around. Some three hundred years

later a new cross, metal this time, was erected to recall the first, in memory of the memory. It is still lit up at nightfall, tracing in the city's sky a kind of crucifix at once spindly and squat, recalling those that until very recently hung, along with sacred images and palm fronds, on the walls of every house in town. Mount Royal is at once a park – laid out by Frederick Law Olmsted, who also designed Central Park in the heart of the island of Manhattan – and a forest. Its slopes give shelter to: three hospitals; two universities; a former philosophy seminary that will soon give way to condominiums; costly private schools with pupils in green and blue uniforms; countless opulent residences whose stone and bricks are covered with hundred-year-old ivy; culs-de-sac lined with small houses that, with their sloping roofs and broad verandas, could have been transplanted from the English countryside. It boasts an artificial lake that has never seen the shadow of a beaver but is populated, winter and summer, by noisy mallard ducks; it was dug on land that once belonged to the Toboggan and Ski Club, where metal posts that once held up the cables of the mechanical lift that took skiers to the summit still stand, supporting pulleys that look like rusty coconuts. Also a restaurant that is all angles, a memory of the 1950s, orange, silver, and yellow; a vast number of big, fat grey squirrels, speedy chipmunks, some foxes, skunks,

field mice, raccoons in the hundreds; radio and cell-
phone antennae stuck into cement bases that look like
bomb shelters; a winding road that opens onto two
lookouts; a third road cut into the rock, once used by a
streetcar and now closed to traffic several times a year
when its shoulders are lined with bales of hay for bicycle
or toboggan races; wooded areas deep in poison ivy,
others where thousands of white trilliums grow, turning
pink, then crimson as the season progresses. At its base
every Sunday a multi-hued crowd gathers, sings dance,
and smoke thin, fragrant cigarettes to the rhythm of tom-
toms and djembes. A few years ago, a second party started
up, and oddly dressed young people in leather or rubber
armour, carrying big cardboard swords that they wielded
peacefully in the undergrowth, flocked from the four corners of the city to wage epic battles between Good and
Evil. Mounted on their good-natured Percherons, the
police stare at both spectacles with the same incompre-
hension. The mountain still shelters the greystone
house of Hosea B. Smith, who bequeathed his land for
a park. It seemed ridiculous: its sides are unassailable,
objected the disgruntled, which drove one Colonel
Stevenson to scale it, twice, in 1862 and again in 1863.
He dragged a cannon with him and fired a series of sal-
voes from the summit that proved beyond a doubt that
it not only was possible to scale the mountain, it could

be done surreptitiously, even if the climber was carrying pieces of artillery. This of course worried the city authorities, who were determined to keep the mountain from being transformed into a Trojan horse, as it were. There is also, at a bend in the road, a slate-roofed pavilion with multiple gables, resembling a small house from a fairy tale and dating from the same period as the now-vanished funicular which led to one of the lookouts; and at the summit, a vast Art Deco structure called, apparently without irony, the mountain "chalet." Its interior is totally empty aside from a snack bar that smells of burnt grease and the sweet odour of sausages sitting in tepid water, and offers the startling sight of a high ceiling supported by caryatids in the form of enormous squirrels. Hidden in the mountain's heart is a reservoir of nearly one thousand cubic metre capacity, its presence announced on the surface only by some narrow pipes that rise out of the ground like periscopes. In every season there are discreet bird-watchers, joggers in head-to-toe Lycra, lovers sharing furtive embraces. Entire immigrant families picnic there in summer, from the wrinkled granny in a shawl and a chignon to the chirping grandchildren around the barbecue where cumin-scented lamb kebabs are grilling. In winter, the slopes are taken over by hordes of little figures in scarves and mittens of every colour, flat on their stomachs on plastic toboggans or old-fashioned

wooden sleighs, holding their breath as they race to the
bottom of the hill.

We talk about her – for it's obvious that by her very
nature she is female – in the singular, but like some
mythological dragon she has three heads, each standing
on guard in turn. She also has labyrinths of paths, stair-
ways, and steep ravines, like a gigantic game of snakes
and ladders.

Her very nicest terrain, where the slopes are gentlest
and offer the eye the most pleasing landscapes, is occupied by four cemeteries, peaceful cities of the dead in the
heart of the metropolis of the living.

It's in the oldest and most densely wooded of these
that he works.

Some of the stones are so old that the name of the person
in whose memory they were erected is illegible, as are the
moment of their birth or the hour of their death. Lying in
the grass, their once-smooth surfaces now covered with
delicate blackish lichen, they resemble flagstones that
trace a winding way into the shadow of hundred-year-old
elms, a garden inhabited by trees and souls.

When she spots him in the distance among the stelae,
the crosses, and the angels with folded wings, he is the
only living being, save for the birds and squirrels that are
the true inhabitants of the place. At this precise moment,

at the sight of his long silhouette standing out against the blue of the sky, she has the impression that he is life itself, that he keeps the garden from foundering into a sleep like the one to which Sleeping Beauty succumbed for a hundred years – or was it a thousand? – that if by misfortune he felt an urge to lie down among the dead, then the Earth would stop turning, the stars would veer off course, the Sun and the Moon would collide.

He watches her arrive, one hand shading his eyes against the blinding light. His cheek and forehead are smeared with brown earth, like war paint. At his feet, spindletrees await planting, roots wrapped in damp burlap. The brass bell of Saint Germain church rings twelve times.

"See what I found this morning when I was digging," he says, taking from his pocket a flat grey stone that she accepts though she doesn't understand. Then, turning it over, she discovers, miraculously, a fish from the depths of time, from the belly of a sea dry now for millions of years, but upon which one can still see each of the fine bones and even the memory of its round eye.

"I'll call him Bubulle," she announces, tracing the jagged outline of a fin.

· · · · · · · ·

Sitting at the foot of the beech tree, each of them is eating half of the sandwich she has brought. The dogs hang around with innocent looks, then leap, jaws clicking, when a bit of bread is tossed to them.

"I have a heart murmur," she announces, not looking at him.

"And?"

"And apparently I have to avoid violent exercise and strong emotions."

"Are you serious?"

"Of course."

"And you can live like that?"

"As you see."

"But what is it anyway, a heart murmur? Something like an air current that runs through it?"

"Not exactly. They say it's congenital. Something about a valve and an atrium. Blood goes in somewhere when it ought to be coming out, or the opposite, anyway something that circulates against the tide."

"You mean there's part of your blood that refuses to go where it should and just does as it likes."

Slightly offended, she retorts:

"I've never seen things that way."

Silence falls between them. Damocles chews conscientiously a tiny piece of ham forgotten by Lili. He makes a new attempt:

"Or else it keeps fighting, even if it's already lost . . ."

Yes, that seems more acceptable. They exchange smiles and for the first time she discovers that one of his front teeth is slightly chipped.

· · · · · · · ·

The earth's core is made up of a blend of iron and nickel. Even today, the exact proportion of the elements that compose it, its behaviour, its effects on the rest of the planet and on the Earth's satellites are still relatively unknown. What is known is that the temperature of the external nucleus is around 4,000 degrees Celsius, that it is liquid and not dense and viscous like magma but has a consistency close to that of water. The waves and tremors that stimulate it create Earth's magnetic pull. But that core conceals another, hard like the stone at the heart of a fruit, whose temperature is some thousand degrees higher. Thus the Earth is like an onion, made up of a certain number of strata of varying thicknesses. We know this thanks to seismological instruments that make it possible to determine the density and composition of these layers by measuring the speed and force of the waves inside them.

What is hidden in the core of the heart no one knows. It has been discovered, however, that its speed of rotation is not exactly the same as that of the planet, a breathtaking observation: the heart and the celestial body spin together in space, with the same movement but at a different rhythm.

At the edge of the clearing grows a clump of birches, their thin trunks gathered together like the stems of a spray of flowers clutched in a hand. The bark of one is ivory, the skin of another a delicate cream that intensifies towards a light beige, a third has shades of pink that verge on cherry-red; together they present an entire palette of flesh tones subjected to the whole range of human emotions, from dread to embarrassment by way of joy.

The young saplings stand brown and pointed like the quills of a giant porcupine that has curled up in a ball and gone to sleep for thousands of years. Low clouds trace long-necked, hunchbacked creatures on the horizon. In the branches, bare for months now, bulges have appeared that resemble large musk strawberries, which crack open, showing green. He came by later than usual, a spade over his shoulder, loping along, afraid she might have left. She offers him a piece of chocolate. A butterfly flutters nervously around them, its wings dark brown, nearly black, edged with white; it seems for a moment eager to touch down on a twig before resuming its pursuit of who-knows-what.

"Did you see that?"

"A butterfly," he observes.

"Yes, but the earth has barely started to thaw, what's it doing here?"

"Who knows? Maybe it's coming back from somewhere."

"But don't butterflies travel in groups? Hundreds of thousands of monarchs all opening out together along the coasts of Mexico then coming back here to gorge themselves on milkweed. Could that one have migrated on its own?"

She looks at the insect circling them, imagining all at once the utter solitude in which it would have had to survive.

"Look," he begins, "it's alive, that's already something, isn't it?"

But she's not certain that it really is a life if it must unfurl in such a desperate search for a fellow creature and not find one.

When she comes back to the cemetery gate the next day, he is waiting for her, smiling. He tells her to sit down, close her eyes, and hold out her hands. She complies unwillingly. He places in her palms a round object, smooth and cold. Opening her eyes she discovers a glass jar with holes pierced in its metal lid, and at the bottom a brown-black butterfly rimmed in white, its straight wings together like hands in prayer.

"See that? I've found another one!"

He seems thrilled at her surprise.

She taps on the glass with her fingernail. She could swear that the butterfly shrugs its shoulders.

"Good for you, but how do you know it's another? How can you be sure it's not the same one?"

"Crap!"

"That's right."

She unscrews the lid, taps the jar to encourage the butterfly to leave. The insect doesn't make a move. Finally, she turns the jar upside down and slaps the bottom. Sluggishly, the butterfly flies away at last.

He looks at her, shamefaced:

"I was so happy to find it, it's crazy, I didn't even think . . ."

"Of course not."

Just then though they both see out of the corner of an eye two dark forms, each the size of a hand, chasing each other near the ground.

"D'you think one of those is the one from yesterday?"

"Who cares? We know at least two of them survived."

The clouds on the horizon part to reveal a patch of sky, a blue window in the surrounding grey. The wind rises and whispers in the branches where the first leaves have come out, bashful and fine, nearly transparent when they emerge from the sheath that served as their cocoon.

"Are you on your own?" he asks without looking at her.

"What do you mean?"

"I mean: have you got a family?"

Damocles, lying at their feet, raises his big head. The other dogs, farther away, are fighting over a ball that squeaks whenever one of them picks it up in its jaws. She takes a branch, its bark already nibbled at by the dogs, and begins to strip its leaves, as if she were removing the petals of a daisy one by one.

"Yes, I have a family. Everyone does, don't they? Unless they're born under a cabbage leaf."

If that is a perch held out to encourage him to open up himself and spare her from answering the question in more detail, he pretends to see nothing and waits patiently for her to go on.

"My parents live in California during the winter, they come back in the spring and move into their house in the Eastern Townships. In good years, we spend a couple of weeks together here, just enough to make me want to hop on a plane as well."

"Why don't you?"

She looks at him as if he had just said something outrageous or dictated by a questionable sense of humour. But apparently the question is serious.

"I hate flying."

"Ah."

At their feet the leaves she continues conscientiously to pull off are piling up, a tiny, soft green mound.

"Is that all?" he asks after a moment.

"Well . . . I mean . . . no. I don't like snakes either or needles. I'm not crazy about pizza and I find the Coen brothers' movies totally uninteresting."

He laughs. Slightly offended, she adds as if to justify herself:

"Their reputation is very overrated you know. They haven't written anything really original since *Barton Fink*."

"I don't know who Barton Fink is and I'm not sure I know the Coen brothers either, but that's not what I meant. I was wondering if you had any brothers and sisters."

"Okay, yes, if I have to tell you everything. A brother two years older than me, Éric. Who, need I mention, loved snakes when he was little, and in his teens ate nothing but pizza."

"Wait, let me guess. He became an acupuncturist, right? Or an airline pilot?"

She smiles in spite of herself and he feels as if he's won an important victory.

"No, an accountant. So's his wife. They live in a reno-vated bungalow in Laval, they play golf, take courses in wine appreciation, and spend two weeks on Cape Cod every summer. What else? They like Swedish mysteries, drive only American cars (on principle, but they do their best, also on principle, to take the Métro as often as possible), and they never go grocery shopping without a dozen reusable bags. Oh, and I forgot, they have 1.4 children."

Now it's his turn to smile.

"Aren't you overdoing it a bit?"

"Not at all. They have a two-year-old little boy who is totally unbearable and Valérie – that's her name, Valérie – is four months pregnant. Do the math."

A cloud sails by, veiling the sun for a moment. A breath of wind lifts a few leaves from the fragile castle at their feet, then the small mound takes off and is scattered almost instantaneously. One leaf glides over their heads before it touches down on the ground between them, where it goes on whirling for a few moments, like a compass needle gone mad.

• • • • • • • •

The cardinals are back. She couldn't say where they come from or when they returned, maybe they spent the winter in the shade of a bird feeder, but it was this morning that she first heard their shrill cheeping, then saw two tomato-red shapes circling each other against the blue of the sky. It is obvious from their scarlet plumage that they are two males, but they don't seem to be chasing one another, rather they appear to be surveying this realm that is theirs, to reconnoitre it and to expand its borders.

She spies the first robins of the season in the middle of the clearing, bellies as round as oranges. Slender buds, their twisted stems like long flames of white and rose can be seen on the cherry tree now. Among the young blades of grass are dozens of blue flowers. All at once she realizes that spring has arrived, that the earth has thawed, and yet there is no sign of the dreaded development whose construction has been suspended for months.

"Why was the work stopped, do you know?" she asks him at noon that day when she spots him at the summit of the mountain, standing near the beech tree.

He gives her an oblique look.

"Didn't I tell you? It was broken off in the light of new information."

"What kind of information?"

To reply he assumes a voice that could not be more official, as if he were presenting the matter to a committee.

"As it happens, this path is home to an endangered bird species, the cerulean warbler, and connecting it with the rest of the network on Mount Royal would have brought more visitors liable to disturb the bird's well-being, not to mention that the work itself would have risked doing considerable harm to its nesting . . ."

She whistles softly. Both sit down, looking straight ahead at the sky that has come to meet the mountains, whose outline can just be made out on the horizon. Not far away, Damocles, intrigued, is face-to-face with a bristling squirrel, tail straight up in the air, pupils blazing, hoisting himself to his full height.

"The cerulean warbler, is that all? And who told the authorities that this ultra-rare species exists?"

He shrugs to declare his ignorance.

"A good Samaritan, of course."

"Of course."

Having apparently decided that the squirrel is an acceptable playmate, Damocles extends his front paws, drops his shoulders so that his chin is almost on the ground, then gives a high-pitched bark. The squirrel responds with an incensed yelping and furiously flicks its tail.

She questions him again:

"Have you ever seen a cerulean warbler?"

"No, but I'm sure I've heard his song, haven't you? Wait . . . Sshh."

He brings his finger to his lips, pretends to prick up his ear. All that can be heard is the wind in the leaves, Juliette delicately peeling a branch, and the spluttering squirrel. Damocles finally turns away, defeated, while the triumphant squirrel wags his tail as one might wave the flag of victory. The dog gives it one last look, then comes and sits at their feet.

"No, I can't hear it," she confesses.

"So maybe we made a mistake," he says, throwing up his hands.

The following day, the posts and the bit of fence have disappeared, leaving in the ground three small shallow holes that Doormat is quick to fill in.

The chestnut tree has started to unfold its big leaves in a kind of backward, slowed-down origami. Half unfurled now, they resemble soft green lilies with oblong petals around a gently swollen tapering core. That stage of false flowering, between bud and leaf, lasts just a few hours. Seeing it very early that morning, as a cloud of mist is coming from the dogs' mouths, she thinks about one of those films that shows in fast motion the germination and growth of a seed lifting its head hesitantly towards the sun.

In the distance, one can see the silhouette of the white big top the circus sets up on the edge of the city every year. It resembles one of the vast tents that Bedouins reserve for their chief in the desert. Spotting the familiar outline, she looks away at once, her heart pounding.

• • • • • • •

It is said that the heart of a man is one and a half times the size of his fist. The bigger that muscle, the more slowly it beats. According to one theory everything that lives and has a heart is granted the same number of beats before it dies – so many for the mouse, so many for the elephant – and once the supply is exhausted, the creature dies. Meaning, perhaps, that the lives of frogs, of hummingbirds and ants aren't really shorter than the life of a man or a whale, but that they unfold at a different rhythm, specific to each species. The length of a life will always be a lifetime; there are planets for example where daylight lasts for months and others where the sun rises and sets every few hours, just as certain ephemeral creatures squeeze into one day what others will take a century to live.

No one knows where or how music was born, or where language originated. It is easy to imagine though that the very first expressions of it (rhythmical clapping of hands or stamping of feet, a piece of wood struck on a stone, then on the taut skin of a drum) were simply repetitions of the beating of our hearts in our chests. If we don't know any animal musicians, ones who make sounds that way to reassure or entertain themselves, or just for the beauty of it, perhaps that's because, unlike humans, they do not feel a need to count out the time that separates them from death.

Music, which can be so precise when expressing sound in its infinite varieties, possesses remarkably few tools when it comes time to take account of silence, which is not its opposite but rather its inverse. The rest sign, a solid rectangular box, a square hat clinging to the fourth line of the staff, corresponds to the whole note and like it, lasts for four beats; the half-rest, equivalent to a half-note, is represented by the same box, this time set on top of the third line where, relieved of half the silence it contained, it could be said to have broken away as it flipped upwards, no longer toppling under its own weight. The quarter-rest, its depiction resembling the profile of a theatre mask with a pointed nose, lasts for one beat, like a quarter-note. The main thing is, it goes no further: each shorter rest is designated by a fraction of the last (half-rest, quarter-rest, and so on) and noted with an oblique line crowned with a kind of slanting comma, which becomes double, then triple and quadruple as needed, the multiplication indicating the shortening of the silence until the stem resembles a spike of goldenrod bending in the wind. With its five small heads the one-hundred-and-twenty-eighth rest is equivalent to the quasi-hemidemisemiquaver. What is there beyond it? Nothing.

Scarcely a breath, the moment that comes briefly before a heartbeat, the rustling of a wing, the fraction of a second between the instant we press the switch and the instant the light goes out, the precise moment when a drop of water suspended from the tip of a leaf breaks away and falls to the ground.

· · · · · · · · ·

It was years ago now, centuries one might as well say, when every night she would go through the movements with a strange sense of moving under water. It would seem to her that she was disappearing, liquefying, leaving room for another woman who knew the motions and whom she watched pirouetting, a spectator of the self who was giving in to the dizziness, then to the brilliance of the leap, fall before flight, and who only made way for her again when it was time to grasp Pierrot's white hand.

Perched on a silver crescent they waited, suspended in mid-air, half-hidden by the darkness that shadowed the summit of the big top, while act followed act in the ring below. Under Pierrot's black hat, his ears, on which he'd forgotten to spread the white chalk, looked like two pink flowers. Columbine briskly caught the trapeze that dropped from the canvas roof. Pierrot followed her slowly, each time leaving the moon reluctantly. This last part of the act, after they'd spent several minutes perched motionless high in the big top, invisible to the spectators, was the most perilous.

—

On the final night, as on all the others, Columbine painted on a round mouth, red as a cherry, long lashes like stars around her eyes. She spied Harlequin behind her in the light-framed mirror. He stopped for a moment at her side; he brushed her cheek with the lace escaping from his velvet sleeve and offered her a cigarette. Dreamily, she took a drag, and smoke floated for a moment above their heads, then dispersed.

The moon, which had been damaged in transport, had been mended, reinforced, sanded, and repainted, but at the junction of the old structure and the aluminium used to repair it there were some rough metal edges that scratched the skin and tore the delicate silk costumes. The whole thing, heated by the floodlights, gave off a smell of paint. Columbine was waiting impatiently to descend to the ring and join Harlequin, whose coloured jacket blazed in the spotlight that followed his every move.

When she realizes that Pierrot won't be able to catch her, it's too late. Did she arrive too soon at the end of the arc traced by her trapeze, or was he just a tiny bit too slow? How to know? The music plays, tinny brasses and ethereal violins, no one can have noticed that their trajectories, which are supposed to cross, will instead brush against one another, then move away again without connecting. She hasn't let go of the bar yet but the movement that will make her do it, already begun, cannot be undone.

The audience, row upon row in their seats, are out-
lined in silhouette, and look as if they've been cut out of
cardboard. Their faces can't be distinguished. As it is
every night, the big top is jam-packed and the ushers
guide spectators to their seats until a couple of seconds
before the show begins. After that they switch off their
flashlights; the narrow beams might distract the performers. Latecomers have to wait for the intermission, standing near the entrances, before they can take their places.

Her fingers release the thin, rubber-coated metal
tube and, briefly, she continues her ascent, carried by the
movement of the trapeze that she's just left.

She sees Pierrot without seeing him. He also knows.
He can do nothing for her.

In the ring, Harlequin, Pantaloon, and the villagers
from whom Columbine and Pierrot have escaped pretend to be searching frantically for them. Armed with
spades and pitchforks, they've emptied a hayloft out of
which burst a host of birds – gracefully skipping contor-
tionists – and, watching their takeoff, the searchers discover overhead the two runaways.

Columbine hears the laughter of hundreds of children whose faces she cannot see. For a moment that is an
eternity, she floats in a kind of weightlessness. At regular
intervals, behind the stands the emergency exits pulse a

vivid red. In the ring, all the characters run around with their heads upturned, they're screaming comically, waving scythes and brooms. The milkmaid's apron is not the colour it usually is; it must have been torn or soiled during yesterday's performance. Golden dust floats in the beam of the spotlights. In the pit the musicians' skulls can be seen, lined up in a semicircle in front of the conductor, a tiny light shining on his rostrum. Four are bald.

Across from her, Pierrot, very close but already insurmountably distant, holds out his arms, stretches his legs, tightens his muscles, his face first distorted by effort and helplessness, then resolute. With a strange near-calm, he lets go, in a final attempt to catch her, because nothing else matters, and if he does manage to grab her he'll find some safe way to land with her in his arms. They both fall like birds cut down in full flight amid the horrified cries of the villagers in the ring. Thinking it's a particularly dramatic finale, the spectators in the stands get to their feet and bring the house down.

Pierrot lands violently in the safety net, has time to feel a spark of pain pass through him from neck to lower back, then faints. Columbine, held back by a harness, is pulled back brutally in mid-fall and stays suspended above him. He can no longer see her. At some point, no one knows when, the music stops.

FOR SEVERAL DAYS NOW DAMOCLES HAS BEEN dragging his paw. He has to be coaxed into or out of the car, hesitates at the bottom of the stairs and at the base of the mountain before he begins climbing with a heavy tread, and if he allows himself to lag behind, it's not always because he's chosen to bring up the rear but sometimes because he has trouble keeping up.

This morning, when she is out of coffee, when she mislays her keys, when she finds a hole in her boot and has to go home and put on an old pair of sneakers that squash her feet, when she turns up late at the house of the university professor who silently hands over his Labradors with an accusing look over his half-glasses, when it starts to drizzle as soon as they finally get to the mountain, the dog's sluggishness exasperates her so much that after berating him one last time, she finally leaves him behind as if in punishment for his lack of will. She advances at a brisk pace surrounded by Vladimir, Estragon, Lili, and Juliette who keep going, barking.

—

It can happen that Lili Lady forgets to pay her for a month, then tries to do so three times in the same week, forgetting every day, it seems, what happened the previous day. Two days earlier, when she brought back the dog, she found the old lady in tears, shaking: "Dear God!" she exclaimed in her slightly lilting accent when she spotted the little white dog on the steps, "Lili! I thought I'd lost you forever!" then shut the door abruptly, without looking up, as if the animal had found her way home on her own after being kidnapped. She doesn't remember the name of the dog-walker but she never forgets the dog's.

The next day she was cheerful and smiling again but she had her sweater on inside out and at the base of her neck, between her hunched shoulders, you could see, standing up like the spring in a mechanical doll, a label with washing instructions. She helped the old lady take it off, then put it back on properly, guiding her frail arms, the skin nearly diaphanous, into the sleeves, as if she were dressing a child.

· · · · · · · ·

"Phhtt," she says, spitting out a little downy ball, "what is this? Did it just appear during the night?"

Around them, the ground is covered with a fine white coating, like after the first snowfall, but this cottony dust flies away at the slightest breath of wind in drifting clouds that float at a low altitude for a moment, then touch down on the grass, flowers, and pebbles. The sky is filled with them, as if the mountain had been the scene of a tremendous pillow fight.

Finally Damocles appears, panting, and lies down between them groaning with relief.

"It's from the white poplars," he explains obligingly, holding out his hand to pick off a small frothy cluster that had formed on her head.

"You mean they moult? That's ridiculous, I've never seen a living being make such a mess in such a short time."

As if to back her up, Damocles produces a spectacular sneeze that sends a little white cloud flying around him. Stunned, the dog seems to be a prisoner of a snow globe. He shakes his head vigorously, long ears flapping in the air, but that only sends up a new plumed cloud from the dirt. He looks up, yawns and hastily shuts his mouth when he feels feathers touching his tongue.

"They aren't moulting, it's their mating season," he explains.

"Couldn't they be a little more discreet?"

"Why would they want to do that?"

She lets out a breath and a small cottony storm is unleashed.

"So what's all that fluff for?"

"It acts as wings for the fertilized seeds and they'll be scattered by the wind . . ."

Another thundering sneeze from Damocles, who scratches his muzzle vigorously with his bear's paw.

". . . and incidentally, by the dogs," he goes on without interruption. "But not all poplars produce it; look."

He points to two trees, identical except that one is wrapped in a fog of fluff balls while the second seems nearly naked in comparison, clad in just its shiny triangular leaves.

"What's wrong with that one, why doesn't it have any, is it sick?"

"It's not sick, it's a male."

She shrugs one shoulder as if to say that she couldn't have put it better.

• • • • • • • •

He also works weekends. She could have sworn it.

Alone with Damocles, she has deluded herself into believing she was taking a walk that would just happen to lead her to the summit of the mountain, and scarcely an hour later she found herself a few metres from him. He waves a greeting, puts down his shovel, and comes to pet the dog, who hails him with joyful trumpeting.

"Do you work nights too?"

"Sometimes. You can't leave plants out of the earth for too long; rosebushes die after no more than twelve hours. And rhododendrons are even more temperamental."

"And there's no one but you to take care of them? Surely you aren't the only employee of this damn cemetery. What if you get sick?"

"I don't get sick easily."

They are sitting in the grass and while he pours the tea, she examines the books that he has, as usual, brought along. A flock of geese crosses the sky, honking noisily.

"Are you a student?"

"Not really. It depends what you mean."

"It isn't complicated: either you're registered at the university or you aren't."

"No, then."

"And all that?" she asks, pointing to the little mountain of books.

"That's the miracle of the library. They give you a card that lets you borrow books and you promise to bring them back."

"You do all that reading for yourself?" Taking the three volumes at the top of the pile, she lists them:

"*Volcanoes: The Character of Their Phenomena, Their Share in the Structure and Composition of the Surface of the Globe.*"

"Histoire du mont Vésuve, avec l'explication des phénomènes qui ont coutume d'accompagner les embrasements de cette montagne."

"Illustrated Guide to the Birds of Quebec."

This last book opens by itself to the page that shows endangered species. She gives him a questioning look and he assumes an innocent expression, explaining: "I'm allowed to have a hobby, aren't I?"

She continues her examination, studying the cover of one last book, worn threadbare:

"Volcanic Studies in Many Lands: Being Reproductions of Photographs by the Author of Above One Hundred Actual Objects, With Explanatory Notices, by . . . wait . . . Tempest Anderson. A prophetic name, don't you think?"

"You forgot this one," he says, turning over the old leather-bound volume he's holding, on which is printed in gilt letters: *An Inquiry Into the Nature and Place of Hell.*

"So you're trying to locate Hell? Most people find it quite easily, don't they?"

"You'd be surprised to know where they place it. Underground. In the sky. On the Sun."

Looking up, he winks as a sign of complicity, with her or with the invisible star beyond the clouds, she couldn't say. The geese shape themselves into two white *V*s, each one seeming to take an already assigned place. Damocles

raises his muzzle towards the sky, surprised by their honking, and answers it with a brief yelp.

She goes on:

"If you aren't a student why all this stuff about volcanoes and earthquakes?"

"I'm leaving soon for a job on the dig at Pompeii. The
least I can do is arrive prepared."

She leans imperceptibly away, squeezes the paper cup
until a nearly unbearable heat spreads over her fingers.

"Right on. Do you speak Italian?"

He looks at her as if it had never occurred to him.

"No. What difference does that make?"

"None at all. You don't speak Italian, but you'll know
precisely where Hell is and what it's made of, so you
shouldn't have any problems."

"That's what I think too."

A breath of wind lifts her hair onto her face, she
pushes it away lock by lock.

"Far be it from me to discourage you," she goes on,
"but hasn't Pompeii already been excavated? I'm quite
sure I've seen photos, maybe even a documentary . . .
You should probably find out before you buy your plane
ticket."

"The dig was started more than three hundred years
ago, broken off, resumed several times, but today there
are still as many buildings buried as exhumed."

"It's not moving very fast," she notes, neutrally.

"Actually it's more and more slowly, because when the buildings are brought into the light, they deteriorate in contact with pollution, even with the air, and also because of the millions of tourists who flood the site every year. Frescoes left perfectly intact for millennia lose their colour in a few weeks; columns that have been standing for two thousand years threaten to crumble."

"So it's more secure underground than in the open air?"

"Well . . . in a way, yes."

"But why try so hard to unearth what's buried if it means putting it in danger?"

The question obviously stuns him. He thinks for a moment, then suggests:

"Most likely there's something more important than security?"

"I see. For instance?"

Again, silence. Then he ventures to say, timidly:

"The open air?"

As she does not answer, he goes on:

"You've never been tempted?"

"To go to Pompeii? Not me. Besides, as I already told you I hate flying."

"Not necessarily Pompeii. Somewhere different. Don't you ever get tired of climbing the same mountain every day?"

She didn't see that one coming, nor did he, and he regrets his words as soon as they've passed his lips. But she has already gotten up. She says over her shoulder:

"If you really think it's the same mountain every day you don't understand a thing."

She drops the cup into the grass where it overturns, and leaves without looking back. After a second of astonishment, Damocles follows her, dignified, all the disappointment in the world in his dog's gaze.

· · · · · · · ·

Sitting at the foot of the beech tree, he rereads for the third time the introduction to a weighty treatise on elasticity written by a distant ancestor. Distracted, he doesn't understand much, raising his head every time he thinks he hears footsteps. Finally Vladimir and Estragon appear, followed by Lili and Damocles, who rears up awkwardly when he spots him and then, limping slightly, nestles his damp nose in the man's neck. But they're accompanied now by someone in his early thirties, hair short, well-dressed but wearing incongruous rubber boots, his manner strangely familiar. He looks at this fellow, puzzled.

The unknown man greets him politely, noting that the dogs are giving him a warm welcome.

"Where is she?" he asks, suddenly concerned.

"In the hospital," replies the other man with no apparent emotion. "Nothing serious, some queasiness last night, but ever since the accident it's best to be cautious so they kept her overnight, under observation."

The close-shaven stranger might as well have been speaking a foreign language. Then he realizes that this man had been with her last evening – though she'd said that she lived alone.

"And you are?" he asks the stranger, resisting an urge to start running.

"Oh, sorry. I'm her brother, Éric," says the other man, extending his white hand.

"The airplane pilot," he murmurs.

"Oh no, not me, I'm an accountant. And . . . umm . . . as my spouse needed a little quiet, I've come to the city for a few days. A kind of vacation," he concludes, sounding like a man sentenced to death. "We had a slight difference of opinion, you see, nothing serious . . ."

But he has already gone. He turns around at the last minute, thinking to ask: "Which hospital?"

Not until he is in front of the imposing brick edifice does he realize that he has no idea what her name is. Strangely enough he's never needed it for thinking about her. Suddenly he is aware that until this morning, he has never spoken to anyone about her, making her all the more precious in his eyes.

But here he is in the entrance to an enormous building where dozens of people are going back and forth, some looking busy, others exhausted: nurses in white or pale green; visitors with unruly children; attendants responsible for this or that, dressed in one-piece uniforms; a few doctors in blue, paper masks around their necks, racing outside for a cigarette or for a coffee at the corner. The lobby reverberates with the clamour of big spaces where people are only passing through: waiting rooms in stations or airports, shopping malls. He sweeps into the first corridor he discovers on his right and tries to remember the elementary principles for exiting a labyrinth. He can't unwind a spool of thread behind him, but turning right whenever he can should let him systematically cover all the floors. And there are probably some departments he doesn't need to go through with a fine-tooth comb: geriatrics, the neonatal unit . . . The thought of it makes him dizzy.

He slowly paces a corridor with a long row of doors on either side, mostly ajar. On the left, pale sunshine leaks out of windows and doorways and stretches across the floor covered with linoleum that's known better days. Overcoming his reluctance and discomfort, he sticks his head in each of the doorways just long enough to distinguish forms stretched out in bed or hunched over in armchairs, near-ghosts that study him for a second, barely surprised, before they go back to their suffering. He doesn't know if he has the will to go on much longer, but he knows that he doesn't have what he would need to leave without seeing her.

She is asleep when he finally locates her room, fourth on the left in the seventh corridor of the west wing on the second floor. Seeing her pale face against the white sheets makes him think of the sunlight on the snow that covered the mountain the day they met. Next to her bed stands a plastic and metal instrument with a black screen where a thin green line traces peaks and valleys, evenly spaced. They remind him of drawings of the periods before earthquakes occur, when the seismograph needle all at once records a number of nearly imperceptible oscillations corresponding to the wavelets, the barely noticeable palpitations and the minuscule eddies that announce the agitation about to shake the heart of the earth.

A tall, thin, sad-faced man is leaving as he arrives. The visitor looks young but he has the eyes of an old man; he leans on a cane as he walks and puts a finger to his mouth, enjoining him not to make any noise.

Silently, he sits in the vinyl chair beside the bed. A feeble light comes in the window and spills, honey-coloured, onto the walls and floor. Sounds from the corridor come to him muffled; the room is strangely calm, as if it has managed mysteriously to detach itself from the hospital and sail upon a slack sea. From his bag he takes a book and his notepad and resumes his reading, turning the pages as gently as he can to avoid disturbing her sleep. She is breathing regularly, like a wave that advances and withdraws under the effect of the backwash. Before long he too dozes off in the warmth of the room.

When she opens her eyes she finds him fast asleep, his mouth wide open. His book has slipped onto his knees and a page has escaped from his notepad. She reaches out for it, unfolds it cautiously. He has noted, in an urgent script:

Augustus Edward Hough Love
Slower than P and S waves, Love waves have a greater amplitude.
It is Love waves that people feel during an earthquake, and Love waves that cause the most damage.

She slips the paper very carefully under her pillow.

Feeling her eyes on him, he wakens almost at once. Jumps up, bends over the white bed. Probes her hazel eyes; in one pupil is embedded a green speck that shines with all the brilliance of the sea on a fine spring day. He would like to place his hand on her forehead but doesn't dare.

"I'm glad you came," she says.

"Me too," he replies, in a tight little voice. He looks tense, runs his hand nervously through his hair to lift a blond lock that has fallen over one eye. His thumbnail is bitten to the quick.

He remains at her bedside all evening and all night, as if he must at all cost prevent sleep from stealing her. He tries to distract her by reading from some gossip magazines he unearthed in a nearby waiting room, then from his ever-present treatise on geodynamics, telling her every story he can think of, asking her the craziest questions, seeking a better way to get to know her than by interrogating her about her past or her sickness:

"If you could only eat one fruit in your lifetime, what would it be?"

"What colour can't you stand?"

"Do you have a favourite star?"

"Do you think it's true that dogs can predict earthquakes?"

After doing her best to answer as honestly as possible (an orange, purple, *Stella Maris*), she looks at him, astounded.

"I should be asking you that, shouldn't I? There must be something about it in one of your books."

"The truth is, scientists have no idea. What's certain is that dogs detect the first vibrations before we do, as if they have a kind of particularly precise seismograph . . ."

"How do they do that?"

"No one knows exactly. It's assumed that they are more sensitive to variations in magnetic fields, so they're more acutely aware of the movement of the magma under the earth's crust. Some believe that perhaps they can pick up very high frequency sounds coming from inside the earth."

"What if they are simply more attentive?"

"Maybe." But he doesn't seem convinced.

"My turn now," she says, raising herself up on her pillows. Her cheeks are tinged with pink, her eyes shining. In the corridors, nurses in rubber shoes go past like ghosts, and pretend not to know that visiting hours have been over for a long time.

"The vegetable you hate?"

"Salsify."

"Favourite animal?"

"Salamander."

"They're supposed to have nine lives, right?"

"No, isn't that cats?"

"You're right. But then how many lives does a salamander have?"

"I have no exact information on that question but I would suggest, without too much fear of being mistaken: just one."

"But aren't they supposed to be legendary animals that are reborn from their ashes?"

"That's the phoenix."

"What about the phoenix?"

"It's the phoenix that is reborn from its ashes. It was said of the fire salamander, *Salamandra salamandra*, that it lived in flames. In *The Travels of Marco Polo*, we read that the shroud of Jesus Christ was preserved in cloth made of salamander."

"How horrible."

"He meant asbestos."

"Why didn't you say so before? Though now that I think about it, that's no more reassuring."

"It's said that salamanders produce a kind of animal asbestos, or maybe asbestos is a sort of plant salamander. The point is that a particularly shrewd scientific mind one day took it into his head to throw a dozen salamanders into the fire to see if they would be magically transformed into some substance dear to the alchemist, if they would produce a fire-retardant thread, or if they would acquire some supernatural power."

"And?"

"They were roasted to death."

"*Sic transit gloria mundi.*"

"They say the same thing was done with witches way back in history. If they were able to avoid being burned at the stake it was proof that they had allied themselves with the Devil. If they burned without a fuss, that proved their innocence and the kingdom of Heaven was theirs."

"And how do you know all that?"

"Doesn't everybody?"

She looks doubtful, then pensive for a moment. The lights of the city sparkle in the window pane, blurred by the rain that has started to fall and to trace long trembling paths on the glass. She suddenly remembers a report she'd seen on TV after a deadly earthquake in China.

"A few days earlier, thousands of frogs had come down from the mountains and overrun the streets. People had to close doors and windows to avoid being infested. The authorities talked about a particularly large migration, about a more abundant population that year, I don't know what other idiotic explanation to reassure the citizens, but of course the frogs were right . . ."

"Appropriately, the first instrument that made it possible to identify the origin of an earthquake was perfected by the Chinese."

"Was it a frog?"

He laughs.

"No . . . Well, actually, yes. More precisely, it was a number of frogs. We had one of those things, very old, at home when I was little; I never knew exactly where it came from or what happened to it . . . Whatever the case, it was a device made up of a kind of big, bronze amphora; all around its sides were eight dragons, heads down, each one with a metal ball in its mouth or, actually, each dragon was supposed to have a ball but it was incomplete and there were only seven. Beneath each dragon was positioned a frog, mouth wide open, ready to receive a ball."

"And the dragons dropped the balls when there was an earthquake?"

"Yes."

"But why eight? Wouldn't one dragon have done the trick?"

"No: the beauty of it is that not all the dragons opened their mouths at the slightest vibration: inside the amphora there was a kind of inverse pendulum that reacted to seismic waves by striking the dragon exactly opposite the direction in which the earthquake was happening."

"So it was one ball that fell . . ."

"Yes and no . . . When the pendulum came back it would also hit the ball directly across from the first one—"

"But tell me, unless there's someone posted permanently in front of it, how could you know if the quake's epicentre was, say, due north or directly south?"

"They didn't know, so the emperor would send riders out on reconnaissance in the two opposite directions, at the same time."

"So the one who found the origin turned back to warn the emperor, that's all right, but how did the other one know that he had to come back?"

"Who said that he came back?"

"You mean he kept galloping non-stop, always moving away from what he was looking for?"

"More or less, yes."

The sun has come up for real, nurses and doctors have started their morning rounds, the shadows of the night have dispersed; he is finally able to believe that she is out of danger.

When he leaves the hospital, without realizing it he takes the road to Saint Joseph's Oratory though he has never gone there before. Once he gets to the enormous grey structure that perches nearly on the summit of Mount Royal, he begins slowly to climb the steps to the crypt. There, he pushes the door to enter a long room, its walls lined with votive lights flickering in their red, green, and yellow glasses, rows of them in tiers like spectators at the circus. The thousands of tiny, guttering candles give off an unpleasant warmth and the smell of wax. Here and there someone slides a coin into a wooden box and the clinking echoes through the room. On the walls between the platforms where the candles are burning hang dozens of wooden crutches and canes, no doubt left by lame pilgrims cured by the Frère André's salutary attentions or the restorative action of Saint Joseph, to whom the sanctuary is consecrated. He shivers at the sight of this collection, unable to stop himself from imagining the mountains of eye-glasses and shoes that inevitably evoke Auschwitz. He reminds himself that this church was built earlier, in a completely different world, where similar mounds were synonymous with miracles rather than the Holocaust. At the base of one of the walls of crutches that have acquired a time-worn sheen, a worker has left behind a pair of work gloves that lie, empty, on the floor.

At the exit from this room there is a door, above which can be read *Information/Benedictions*. Glancing inside, he sees a peculiar silver object, half-cooking pot and half-samovar, crowned by a panel declaring *Holy Water*. Next to it is a box filled with miniature plastic bottles like those allowed on airplanes.

He wanders aimlessly through the maze of corridors and stairs that lead from one room to another, and soon finds himself in a hallway where, tucked deep in an alcove cut into a wall and protected by a grille, a brownish object that might have been a stone is exhibited in a small glass reliquary. On the heavy metal doors can be read:

> *Here rests in the peace of God*
> *the heart of Brother André, C.H.S.,*
> *founder of the Oratory, 1845–1937*

At the foot of the marble pedestal holding the glass box are a few scraps of paper with prayers or thanks scribbled on them and some coins, as if thrown by someone making a wish at a fountain. Not far away water is flowing. Letting the sound guide him, he comes to a long, concealed corridor that seems to have been dug out of the mountain and sees that he is standing opposite a rock wall covered here and there with green moss. Droplets fall from the rock face as if from an immense stone cheek, one by one with a sound like rain.

A series of escalators similar to those in shopping malls leads to the basilica, which he eventually reaches though he doesn't know it, for want of reference points. He hasn't seen a window to the outside for a long time and he feels as if every footstep is taking him deeper into the heart of the mountain. Finally he pulls open some heavy doors to enter a room so vast that for a moment it takes his breath away. There is no natural light here either, aside from some scarlet rays darting in through stained-glass windows that seem to have been shattered and stuck back together in a hurry. He advances towards the choir, his footsteps ringing out on the floor. Here and there he can make out a stooped figure seated on a long wooden bench. The entire nave, seemingly made of cement, is reminiscent of the architecture of early twentieth-century dams whose double purpose was to subjugate nature and to declare loud and clear man's superiority over everything around him. No doubt here it is meant to exalt the greatness of God, but the effect is the same. He recalls that Brother André was a small man, five feet tall at most, a humble porter.

On either side of the choir the apostles stand in groups of three, looking aghast and inevitably suggesting the three monkeys who see nothing, hear nothing, say nothing. Behind the altar rises a monumental wooden cross; the tortured Christ is flanked by Mary and Mary Magdalene, faces downturned, hands raised, apparently lamenting some tragedy that has occurred on the ground during the execution of the Saviour. Huge rectangular light fixtures hanging from the ceiling cast a cold light into the apse. Going closer, he notes a bouquet of red roses at the foot of the altar and he kneels in front of them: of all the things in this place, they alone are still somewhat alive. The paving under his knees is icy and when he gets up he limps a little.

It is on his way back down, upon turning onto a corridor, that he discovers Brother André's tomb, an enormous black marble sarcophagus, perfectly plain, concealed in a peculiar semicircular room lined with brown bricks. He stops in front of the dark block, trying to imagine the body resting there, with a hole in place of the heart.

THIS MORNING, THERE IS A SMALL CROWD outside Lili Lady's house. She is being escorted by two middle-aged women who might be her daughters or social workers, she can't guess from their manner, at once professional, efficient, and somewhat appalled. Each is holding one of the old lady's elbows; Lily Lady is pretending to try to free herself but seems nearly happy at the attention.

"Martha!" she exclaims, spotting her across the street, "Martha dear, I'm going on vacation! On a transatlantic liner, no less. They've promised me a cabin with all the modern conveniences."

One of the women slowly shakes her head while the other rolls her eyes. "Come now, just another few steps," whispers the first one, pointing at the car that's waiting, door open. The old lady gets in, smiling broadly, waves through the window with a small dignified gesture, fingers slightly curled, palm cupped, like the queen in her carriage. Just then there is barking from inside the house and

Lili Lady's face contorts first in surprise, then in sorrow. She opens her mouth in a silent cry, rests her forehead on the window, and closes her eyes while the car moves off.

The door to the house is still open; a man comes out, moustached, carrying an attaché case and holding a leash with Lili at the end of it, straining, standing on her hind paws, struggling and producing high-pitched yelps.

"Where are you taking her?" she asks the man, who is busy locking up.

He looks at her for a moment, then says grimly:

"Where d'you think? A luxury dog hotel?"

"Not the dog, the woman, where are you taking her?"

"Are you a relative?"

"What difference does that make?"

"What's your name?"

"You heard, it's Martha."

"Martha what?"

"None of your business."

She holds his gaze. He has brown eyes and one eyelid that quivers faintly when he speaks.

"And the dog – where are you taking her?"

He stares at her without replying, furious, his moustache trembling; it's almost as if he is taking pleasure in this exchange. She tears the leash from his hands and turns around before he can say a word. Lili, head down, obediently follows.

· · · · · · · ·

For the first time they are side by side facing the river, and being together in front of the promise of this immense expanse is both dizzying and reassuring. The wharves are deserted, everything is soaked in a fine grey rain that forms a ghostly halo around the huge rusty ships, some seeming to have been anchored there for years, looking like part of the landscape; the huge empty hangars; the nearby bulk of the old grain silo with broken windows from which flocks of slate-coloured pigeons emerge; and Île Sainte-Hélène where you can barely discern the outline of the condominiums piled one on top of the other with no apparent logic, like wooden cubes stacked by a child. The entire Vieux-Port is deep in the heart of a cloud.

The water laps gently, licking the low cement wall they are leaning against in the hope of spotting a fish she thinks she saw flash silver. But the river is murky, opaque as milk, and grey. They stay there for a long moment, now and then the haunting cry of a gull pierces the silence and gives a fleeting impression of the seaside. When they raise their heads the fog has cleared.

"The cloud has passed," she notes, surprised.

"Or we have," he retorts, surprising her even more.

The rain has stopped, leaving the asphalt gleaming like a mirror. In Old Montreal they take streets paved with small, round, uneven cobblestones, walking past the Bonsecours Market, its silver dome, pierced with windows, resembling a stocky lighthouse, then they start the climb towards the mountain along St. Lawrence Boulevard, which begins at the river of the same name and joins the Rivière des Prairies at the far north end of this strange island where water is rarely visible. River and boulevard have been baptized in honour of an iconoclastic third-century martyr, abducted as a small child, then found under a laurel, the tree to which he owes his name. At the end of his life, laid out to be roasted on blazing coals by his torturers, instead of shedding useless tears, Lawrence announced after a few minutes that he was well done on one side, they could turn him over. Against hatred, stupidity, and death he set the quiet strength of his clear laughter, silencing his executioners' hilarity with the fearsome laugh of the victim. In an irony so great that it can also be seen as a kind of homage, he was named the patron saint of *rotisseurs*. Be that as it may, in 1672 in this land of New France, they had actually named what was still just a modest dirt path "Saint Lambert's Way," not, as one might think, in honour of Saint Lambert – who had died in the year 700, with a lance through his heart, when standing at the altar in the chapel of Saints Cosmas and Damian in Liège – but rather in memory of Lambert Closse, who lost his life in 1662 while defending

Ville-Marie against an Indian attack, with the help of his dog, Pilote.

Since the eighteenth century, it has united and separated the city at once, just as the arteries starting at the lungs irrigate the body besides delimiting the main zones. Still today, Saint Lawrence Boulevard is the dividing line from which, going both west and east, street numbers are counted starting at zero, a kind of Greenwich meridian, Montreal style. That "Main" (for a time known as Saint-Lawrence-of-the-Main, which a particularly ill-advised translator of Mordecai Richler once rechristened "rue principale") acts as the demarcation line between the two halves of the island: affluent Anglos on the west, perched on the hills of Westmount, and working-class French on the east, whose poverty spread in the past to inner suburbs similar to those described by Gabrielle Roy in *The Tin Flute*. Both territories are now mixed, hybrid, confused, though the border is still there, memory or warning.

At the corner of de la Gauchetière, lacquered ducks, red and glossy, hang by their necks, heads falling gracefully to the side as if they were asleep. In the windows are stacks of small wooden and porcelain cases, flasks and flagons, roots, dried leaves, powders, balms, and ointments whose mentholated odour spreads to the street. Crates of oddly shaped fruit, some with brown spots, others bristling with sharp spines, are unloaded at the doors of shops that sell blue-and-white teapots, dried shrimp, bubble tea, and smoked eel.

Beyond René-Lévesque (which, a few kilometres west, in Westmount, is still called Dorchester) is a new country, no more than a few blocks long, where only yesterday the Frolics, then the Roxy, the Midway, and the Crystal Palace were established; now all that is left to bear witness is the Café Cléopâtre. As early as 1819, this section of the street counted twice as many taverns as grocery stores. Girls teetering on high heels, some of them not exactly girls, will spend the night in the doorways of snack bars where hotdogs, *steamés* or *toastés*, are cheap, waiting for a car to stop near them, hearts pounding from withdrawal and fear. Inside, the leatherette banquettes and the orange tables where people sit to eat poutine are bright under the fluorescent lights; outside, the street is grey where shadows glide.

Sometimes, at dawn in those alleys a girl will be found, covered with bruises, left there among the plastic cutlery, abandoned syringes, and sticky condoms. At this time of day the street is practically deserted. A homeless man sitting in the entrance to an ATM is petting his dog, lying curled up at his side; teenagers run up the slope to Sherbrooke Street. Farther away, they pass without a word into the realm of bling, of exorbitant restaurants and bars where every evening long lines of people stand, stamping their feet as they talk on their cellphones and where, some claim, just the night before, they saw Robert De Niro or Leonardo DiCaprio. In parking lots resembling second-hand luxury car dealers, brightly shining cars with sparkling chrome will line up; from them will emerge long-legged girls, girls who could be the sisters of those glimpsed, staggering, a little lower down on the street, in the doorways of greasy spoons reeking of rancid oil, accompanied this time by thick-haired men with heavy steel watches who laugh loudly and seem when they speak to be addressing an invisible audience. The restaurants will fill up; against a background of deafening music people will be served dishes with complicated names that will include chorizo, gravlax of something or other, and Kobe beef, often on the same plate, sometimes impossible to tell apart, served by statuesque but thoroughly morose models. At this hour, however, their windows are empty, black, and blind.

It was there on this thoroughfare that more than a hundred and fifty years ago, Guilbault's Botanical and Zoological Garden spread out in all its splendour. Its spectacular grounds first opened in 1840; the various attractions (greenhouse, an area planted with fruit and forest trees, gymnasium) could be visited for the sum of precisely seven and a half pence. According to the proprietor, gathered together there was "one of the largest collections of live wild Animals, rare Birds and Natural Curiosities in North America." Depending on their inclination, visitors could take home a horticultural or avian souvenir, because "dahlias, roses, poultry, birds" were offered with equanimity.

As for feathered creatures, store fronts in the Portuguese neighbourhood proudly display multicoloured pottery roosters at their doors and restaurants that serve up golden, spit-roasted chickens, whole fried fish, and good strong coffee; just a little further up and set back slightly from the street, there is a tombstone company; another that's been selling cut-rate shirts for decades; cabinet-makers and second-hand stores that are to some degree the memory of this boulevard that is itself the city's memory. Designers' studios, vintage clothing boutiques, and everything in between (recycled, mended, new clothes made from old rags); a vegan restaurant where butter is replaced by sesame paste and bacon by seitan; farther north, a bar without a name or sign, its logo a little bird drawn on a slate with chalk that Anglos call "Sparrow" while for Francos it's "Moineau." Nearly across the street, another restaurant called Lawrence in honour of the boulevard, where you can eat *bubble and squeak* as if in an English cottage; a brick building that is home to hundreds of twentysomethings in fair-trade cotton T-shirts and Converse sports shoes, busy creating video games, while across the street is a bright café with big windows where one can drink tea peacefully in the afternoon surrounded by plants. It is there that they leave the Main, which continues on its way to the tip of the island, stopping only when the street finally finds water again.

THE MOUNTAIN IS COVERED NOW WITH A TENDER green shadow, scarcely more than a shiver, a shimmer at ground level and at the tips of branches, a shadow that spreads from day to day until the mountain is totally enveloped. Clusters of miniature seed pods, nearly translucent, hang by the handful from maple twigs, dazzling tulips have opened in the undergrowth – how they got there no one knows – forming bright red bells on the dark earth.

The summit this morning is bathed in a fine mist that might be rising from the earth or falling in a drizzle from the clouds. The sky is the grey of felt, and the droplets look like a thousand cold needles. All that's visible of the Saint-Germain church is the pointed tip of the verdigris steeple. One can't even hear the birds that are taking shelter from the rain, nestling near the trunks of the most verdant trees. She is alone in all that fog, along with the soaking wet dogs and their dirty paws.

Not until she is getting ready to go home does she realize Damocles hasn't rejoined them. She calls once, twice, three times. Lili, who hasn't left her side for days, pricks up her ears and looks at her, distraught, then spins around and races down the path, kicking up arcs of mud behind her slender paws. She turns immediately and follows the dog, at first briskly, then at a trot, ultimately running as fast as she can, whistling, calling again. She can no longer feel her legs, feels almost as if she is flying, and all at once it seems to her that there'll be no end to this descent. Finally she spots the heavy shape lying on the edge of the path. He tries awkwardly to get up as she approaches but, too feeble to hoist his body on his long legs, the animal falls back on his knees and chin, only able to wag his tail.

The dogs stop behind her, at a respectful distance. In the dirt she sees the hesitant traces Damocles has left, the outline of his big body on the ground, his wobbling steps, again the impression of his flank on the earth. He has fallen and pulled himself up as many times as she has called him.

He is panting with effort, has trouble holding up his head, which she takes and gently settles on her knees. He follows her every move with his big eyes which express his despair; he wants to obey but can't. "Good dog," she murmurs, and a nearly transparent membrane briefly covers the black pupil. Damocles raises an ear. He lets out a groan that expresses as much surprise as suffering. She strokes the soft hair of his ear, his warm nose, smoothes his forehead and his worried eyebrows; a quivering begins in his cheeks and runs through the dog's entire body. His pink mouth opens; his tongue is hanging out, he doesn't stop looking at her and uses whatever strength he still has to keep his eyes open. Softly she says: "We'll soon be home, old pal." Only then do his brown eyes close. The head on her knees is heavy, like a stone.

The dogs approach now, sniffing Damocles' remains as they might some unknown object. From her own throat comes a moan that she doesn't recognize either.

· · · · · · · ·

The two shaky flashlights make holes in the night, two delicate white tunnels where big white moths and other pale butterflies with large blind eyes flutter, panic-stricken, tiny, ephemeral, nocturnal fauna irresistibly attracted by the light.

It takes forever to dig, at the foot of the beech tree, the grave where gently he places Damocles, who from now on will be one with the tree. She has brought a blanket, a bone, and a teddy bear missing two arms and a leg that the dog used to carry delicately in his teeth as if it were some precious, fragile treasure. Kneeling on the cold ground, she throws handfuls of earth onto the body of Damocles, who looks as though he is sleeping.

The moon rises, huge and white on the horizon, casting an ashen light on the rocky mountainside and on the city below. The North Star sparkles above the trees. On drowsy Mount Royal all that can be heard is the wind rustling in the leaves and now and then, the surprised hoot of an owl. When the grave is filled in, she carefully chooses each of the pebbles and puts together a dog made of stones, lying on its side, holding in his mouth a teddy bear.

They stay there for a long time, between the lights of the city and the wealth of stars. At the same moment, elsewhere on earth as well as nearby, children are dying and forests are burning, men strike other men who are their brothers, or their wives, or their daughters, while on all sides cries of distress rise up in the night. They both stay there, crying over the death of a dog.

Then the moon disappears at the same time as the wind rises, as if chased away by the breeze. Leaves turn, rustling, showing their grey undersides. A droplet lands on her shoulder, another on her nose and soon the storm is raging. The drops fall so heavily now that they draw long oblique lines in the air like those traced in the sky by shooting stars. They can see nothing even two steps away, the air is saturated with moisture, erasing the outlines of tombstones and the horizon, all lost in the leaden grey of the storm. A distant lightning flash lights up a patch of sky, followed by a muffled crackling. At the first drops he tried to pull her blindly down a winding road lined with vaults like massive sentinels. A new flash of lightning illuminates with a brief white brilliance trees and tombs, followed at once by a deafening roar, as if the sky had split in two.

She throws up her arms towards the clouds, throws back her head, closes her eyes. The distance separating the intensity of the flash from the rumbling of thunder diminishes each time, as if after having followed it in vain since the dawn of time, the roar was finally able to catch up with the light.

"Come on," he urges her, but she doesn't move, her face flooded.

He takes her elbow, tries to pull her; she frees herself. Now the lightning is sweeping the sky like spotlights, while the rumbling thunder makes the ground vibrate beneath their feet. Frantic, he looks for a shelter close by.

He did not see the thunderbolt fall but he felt it, a tremendous discharge that in an instant brings together sky, fire, and earth. A powerful smell of ozone spreads through the damp air. The oak where they picnicked more than once splits in two from top to bottom with a grim creaking sound; one emaciated half of the tree, festooned in black, still stands. The inside of the tree was hollow.

After that she lets herself be led docilely to a stone vault. He pushes a heavy bronze door that opens without a sound, revealing a dark interior where they can discern some long rectangular forms arrayed on thick stone shelves.

The candle lights up one side of his face and she has the impression that she can make out better than ever before the bridge of his nose, the curve of his chin, the line of his cheekbones, and the tiny creases that form at the corners of his eyes when he smiles, as if until now, daylight and lamps have always hidden some part of him that is only revealed in this chiaroscuro.

He clears his throat as if preparing to say something but remains silent, finally sitting on the ground, hugging his knees as he leans against the wall at his back. Looking up, he pats the earth in front of him and she comes and nestles between his legs, her back against his collarbone. He puts his arms around her waist, and through the layers of soaking-wet cloth she can feel the warmth of his body. His breath is warm and regular on her neck, then on her lips, her shoulders, her belly.

They stayed in the mausoleum for hours, the candle warming the darkness. She woke up just before dawn and watched him, still asleep, half-undressed, their clothing rolled up in a ball. Eyes closed, lips parted, he looked like a statue. During the night a young and slightly prickly beard had covered his cheeks. She pulled on the door. The rain had stopped and on every blade of grass stood drops, round and trembling. A green odour rose from the earth, the sky in the east was turning pale while the stars that had reappeared during the night were declining one by one in the burgeoning light. All around her the dead were sleeping while in the city the living were slowly waking up.

He emerges from the tomb, dishevelled and still numb with sleep, at the same time the sun rises.

"My name is Rose," she says, without turning around.

"And I'm William, Love."

She smiles. Of course his name is Love. In front of Rose Cyparis and William Love, the first light of dawn is stretching out between the graves. The silence suggests that the earth has drunk up the last sound and is dozing still, peacefully, in the veils of night. The nocturnal animals have hidden themselves from the daylight; there'll be no visitors for a long time. A crow spreads its wings and takes flight. The cemetery belongs entirely to the still stones marking the presence of the dead, some with the appearance of a standing man, erected in memory of those who lived – a day, a hundred years – on this earth to which their bodies have been committed and with which they are now one. The rays grow longer, spangled with gold, next to the silhouettes of the crosses and statues lying on the ground where shadow and light rest together.

ACKNOWLEDGEMENTS

I hope that historians, mathematicians, geologists, and other experts will not hold against me the liberties I have taken with their respective fields. While inspired by facts, this book is a work of the imagination.

It seems that Baptiste Cyparis (who has also been called Ludger Cyparis, Louis-Auguste-Cyparis, and Jean-Baptiste Sylbaris) was in fact the only human to have survived the deadly eruption of Mount Pelée on May 2, 1902, in the course of which some 30,000 lives were lost. Following that "achievement," he was apparently recruited by the Barnum & Bailey Circus and became one of the main attractions in its traveling show. Not much more is known about him, but anyone wishing to learn more about Saint-Pierre at the time of the eruption may consult *Fire Mountain*, by Peter Morgan. Readers will find in it a rigorous chronology of the events – from which I have allowed myself to depart. Information relating to the first excavations at Pompeii was mostly taken from *Pompeii Awakened*, by Judith Harris.

The mathematician August Edward Hough Love, born in 1863, was interested in geodynamics and the elasticity of solids, fields in which he made significant discoveries. His career at the University of Oxford was longer and more brilliant than the one I created for him in London. *Love numbers*, named in his honour, are used to measure the elastic response of the Earth to the influence of the tides, and *Love waves* are still used today in studying the Earth's crust and, especially, earthquakes. I made Edward Love a few years younger and created for him the imaginary existence that his real name seemed to call for. I like to think he wouldn't have minded.

• • • • • • • •

Many thanks to Nadine Bismuth, François Ricard, and Yvon Rivard, first readers who are at once shrewd and benevolent. Thanks to Dr. Danielle Gilbert, who saved me from committing absurdities in *materia medica*. Thanks to Julie Robert, Éric Fontaine, and Éric de Larochellière. Thanks to Antoine Tanguay, monsieur Alto, for his fiery spirit, his intelligence, and his passion for literature. Thanks to Lara Hinchberger for her instincts and her keen eye, to Ellen Seligman for a wonderful title, and to Sheila Fischman for lending her talent to my book.

Finally, thanks to Victor the dog for the daily walks on the mountain that now reminds me of him each time I see it. And thanks to Fred for everything – and all the rest.

A NOTE ON THE TYPE

Wonder is set in a digitized form of Caslon, a typeface based on the original 1734 designs of William Caslon. He is generally regarded as the first British typefounder of consequence and his designs continue to be widely considered among the world's most readble text faces.

The display font is Zebrawood, a "woodtype" adapted from mid-nineteenth-century circus posters and handbills.